BUSHWOOD MURDER

AUGUSTA MYSTERY

For Dad and Chum; Dick and Esther; Scott and Gummer;
Jim and Skip; Slacks and the Fly; Longshanks and Hawker;
Bunny and Huck; Dan and Doug; BT and Marky Mark;
Amy and Rich; Vegas and Rocco; Bwana and Chewie;
Larry and Tutchi; Killer and Mo; Goose, Dino, and Rube;
Bitch Slap and the Rake; Oregon John and Big Smooth;
Shambone, Rusty, and Ben; Bad Billy, Andy, and Chuck;
Four Putt and the Wiz; Jaws, Grandpa, and Shanks Ladue;
Spud Boy and Raymundo; Jaco and Skunk; Ravi and Thor;
Angel and NetZero; Byron and ScottO; Dougie and JD;
Reno, Skipper, Air, Dingle, Plato, Jammers, and Rooster;
Ringo and Puker aka the Mouth that Roars; and for all the
other brothers and sisters out there along life's fairways.

Golf is a study in our greed

as well as our lack of faith.

John Updike

Golf is played at many levels.

Michael Murphy

One: Dougie
Members Practice Area
Augusta National Golf Club
Augusta, Georgia

Smails. Everything always came back to Judge Smails. The walk from the clubhouse past Magnolia Lane down to the members practice area was sublime. The sun rising out of the mist over Ike's Pond was surreal. There was nobody else on the range. It was one of Dougie's great joys, having the whole range to himself early in the morning. But even now, even here, even more than ever, Dougie felt the Judge looming over him. It made it hard for him to relax or focus or even think about anything else.

Dougie pulled two clubs from his bag and began stretching in the warm April morning air, hoping his warm-up routine would settle him. He always started with his eight and nine irons. First he held both clubs together overhead between his hands and stretched as tall as he could, extending his spine to the sky. Then he started bending slowly down to his left and right, cautiously moving his low back gently around in circles as his shoulders rotated and he loosened his core muscles. He held one iron out in front of him with each hand and slowly rotated his wrists back and forth while he stretched his legs, crouching up and down and feeling his center balance. Then he settled into his stance and started letting his arms move around, pulling his shoulders back and forth. Before he knew it, he was swinging the clubs in parallel, his eight

1

iron with his left side and the nine iron in his right hand. When he could feel both clubs, both sides of his body, flowing effortlessly together back and forth in tempo and on plane, he knew he was ready to play golf.

Then, like Tiger and Jack, his first few shots of the day were soft little half-swing eight irons. He gradually worked up to full swings. He stopped warming up and started hitting golf shots. Next he dropped "down the wheel," that's what Jack called it, playing every other club in his bag until he got to his driver. He hit nine drives, visualizing and executing the nine different tic-tac-toe combinations of high, low, and medium draws, fades, and straight drives that Tiger popularized working with Hank Haney. Dougie's dad told him once that Hogan learned that drill from Jimmy Demaret and taught it to Lee Trevino. Finally, he came back "up the wheel" one club at a time, visualizing and executing specific shots he expected to play today. He'd done essentially the same thing, the same way, as best he could, before every round of golf he'd played for the last 55 years. He'd done it that way ever since the first week of golf practice in seventh grade when a runty little barrel of energy in crisp new plus-fours named Elihu Smails crashed into his life.

Sometimes Dougie couldn't remember ever doing anything without the Judge. Sometimes he wondered whether Smails had even really been in all the memories Dougie had of him. Sometimes he'd remember things he was sure happened in third or fourth grade and swore he saw the Judge there, eating cheap store-bought birthday cake at parties far below his social orbit. Maybe, he thought, the Judge's personality was so strong that even Dougie's memories were shaped by his indomitable will, just like the rest of his life had been.

Dougie focused, relaxed, visualized, and executed a three-quarter six iron. It carried about 145 yards with a soft draw. At his age, Dougie only hit full shots when he absolutely had too. Even when he'd been younger and stronger, he'd never tried to overpower much of anything, much less something as big as a golf course. That had served his game, if not always the rest of his life, pretty well over the years. The Judge, for his part, tried his whole life to overpower everything and everyone who ever stood in his way. It turned him into a hack and a cheat who never honestly broke 80 even once, but it made him one of the most powerful men in Western Nebraska.

Now Judge Smails was dead. Murdered. Someone shoved a shower-curtain rod down his throat. The coroner said he'd laid there dead, naked on the floor of his marble-tiled walk-in shower, for three or four days. They'd just found his body last Friday. His landscaper, Milo Holy Rock, called the police late that afternoon. The Judge hadn't left Milo's check and wasn't answering his door or his phone. The cops broke through the gates later that evening and forced open the huge double doors. Word spread quickly after they found the Judge's body.

According to Chief Riggs, who'd given Dougie a full report on the Bushwood driving range Sunday afternoon after his first round of the year with the Mayor's crew, there were no signs of struggle, forced entry, or robbery. "It was somebody he knew," Riggs told him as they stood there pretending to hit wedges. "Or it was some kind of professional assassin. And it was nasty. The Judge did not die well."

Dougie didn't want to hear the gory details—he knew Chief Riggs was only too ready to share them—and he was pretty sure there weren't any professional assassins in North Platte. There were only about 30,000 people in town. The richest and most influential were all, almost without exception, Bushwood members. He'd been a shop assistant, the Bushwood club pro, and now since the start of the year the teaching pro emeritus, for a little more than 45 years. He knew a lot of secrets. None of them involved murder.

This trip was supposed to be his semi-retirement present from the club. It was Smails, of course, who'd organized it. As usual, Bushwood went along with the Judge. The board dutifully voted to cover their airline tickets, hotel rooms, and rental vans. Dougie and his younger brother Danny visiting Augusta the week before the Masters with Smails and three of the Judge's long-time Bushwood cronies. Two rounds at "the National," as

Smails called it with his trademark deep chuckle, not so subtly reminding everyone within earshot that he knew not one, but two members.

"One last trip with the good old boys," the Judge promised in his presentation at Dougie's retirement dinner last December. They'd visit steakhouses and Waffle Houses, the Judge said. They'd play golf under the Georgian sun; they'd share golf stories; they'd laugh like they were young. "Or at least a little younger, eh?" the Judge quipped, unleashing the cackle of laughter he reserved exclusively for his own jokes.

Smails' death wasn't very funny. There hadn't been much laughter on their trip. Dougie had expected everyone to just cancel the whole thing. On Monday, he'd been the one who'd reached out to their hosts, Charlie Kellerman and Miles Postlewaite, to tell them about the Judge. He'd heard the Judge tell the same five or six stories about his law school exploits with "Chucky and Smiley" for more than forty years, but he'd never actually met either of them. They both lived in tony Connecticut suburbs and worked for powerful New York law firms in tall buildings where neither of them, as the Judge always said, ever had to risk the indignity of going to court. As far as Dougie knew, neither of them ever suffered the indignity of visiting the Judge in North Platte either.

He'd expected Chucky and Smiley to be distraught over the death of their law school comrade. But as far as

Dougie could tell on the phone, their main concern seemed to be the inconvenience the Judge's passing threatened. They'd both strongly insisted on sticking to their schedule. "A deal's a deal," Postlewaite told him twice. It seemed a really cold way to talk about a golf trip, but Kellerman intimidated that cancelling their rounds at the National on such short notice—days before the Masters—would be socially awkward. Everyone in golf knew how arcane and unyielding the ruling powers of that club could be. But it was still more than a bit off-putting how little remorse the Judge's old law school buddies expressed over the phone. Their hosts hadn't even introduced themselves yet and Dougie was already a little unsure about playing with them.

The Judge's three Bushwood cronies glommed onto Chucky and Smiley's story in about a heartbeat when Dougie told them about his phone calls. None of them seemed particularly out of sorts, or said anything about cancelling. They all made a point of saying "that's what the Judge would have wanted" two or three times. Dougie felt a little sad three guys who'd played with the Judge several times a week for ten or fifteen years weren't a bit more upset about his murder.

But he wasn't entirely surprised. All three of them had complained to Dougie about the Judge dozens of times. Cheating, not paying his bets, lying, making passes at wives: Smails had plenty of bad habits. And the Judge told endless stories about his rounds "at the National with

Chucky" or "when Smiley and I were in Augusta" at the drop of a hat. Those guys heard every one of his stories hundreds of times. But in all those years, Dougie never once heard of the Judge taking any of his Bushwood buddies to the Georgia pines. This would be their one and only chance to play Augusta. Not a one of them had any inclination to pass that up out of respect for the dearly departed Judge Smails. He'd done them all wrong more than once. They'd kept playing along with him, and this trip was as much payback as any of them was ever likely to get.

Dougie knew a lot of people despised the Judge. He'd never imagined any of them would shove a shower curtain rod down his throat and leave him to bleed out on his bathroom floor. "It was somebody he knew," Chief Riggs said. Dougie just couldn't believe it. He couldn't even imagine anyone being in the bathroom while the Judge took a shower. Not even his first wife, Pookie, before she passed. He wasn't sure why. Dougie just couldn't imagine Smails being that intimate with anyone, even his wife. Dougie certainly never would have shared a bathroom with the Judge and he'd probably spent as much time with Smails as anyone besides his wives.

Dougie was never really sure whether or not he'd ever been the Judge's friend. "My golf pro," that's how Smails always introduced Dougie. Never "my friend, Bushwood's golf pro" or "my friend Dougie—he's the golf pro at

Bushwood." Just "my golf pro." Dougie had no doubt that if he wasn't any good at golf, or if he hadn't run Bushwood so well, the Judge would never have spent so much time with him or played such a leading role in his life. And their "friendship" was pretty businesslike when it came right down to it. It was firmly rooted at Bushwood. It didn't spread far beyond the club. Dougie could count on one hand the number of times the Judge had visited his house. He wasn't sure the Judge could have picked any of his three daughters out of a lineup.

Somehow it all made Dougie feel guilty. He knew how much the Judge loved Bushwood, and how much he loved golf, in his own strange way. And inside his small narrow world, the Judge had clung ferociously to his vision of their friendship ever since that fateful seventh grade meeting on the sun-baked rubber mats at the old River's Edge driving range. Now, standing on the immaculately-groomed turf of one of the most legendary ranges in the world, trying to prepare mentally and physically to play one of the great courses for the first time, Dougie kept feeling in the pit of his stomach the harsh realization that the Judge had never really been his friend. His grief was turning that into guilt, even though it was the Judge, not Dougie, who'd never been able to have a real friendship.

They'd certainly never been equals on the golf course, which mattered a lot more to the Judge than it ever did to Dougie. But they'd never really been equals off the course either. And that also mattered a lot more to Smails. You couldn't build a meaningful friendship on a foundation like that, Dougie thought, where one person was so determined to catch up with and stay ahead of the other. Friends didn't build over the top of each other, they built each other up.

But Smails was so driven and so passionate. The Judge always knew exactly what to do. It never really seemed to make much difference what anyone else thought, or did, or said. Smails had so much energy and so much confidence that if you weren't careful, if you hesitated at all, you'd spend forty years doing what he wanted before you stopped and caught your breath. Was that what got him killed? Had he finally pulled the wrong string on the wrong person?

Like any older golf pro, Dougie had seen and heard about his fair share of lies, cheating, betrayal, and treachery. But never murder. There were about four murders in North Platte every decade, Chief Riggs told him. Every murder the Chief could remember resulted from the same deadly combination of alcohol and domestic violence. In all those cases, the Chief said, they knew whodunit before the body ever hit the morgue.

Riggs had been the Chief for almost twenty years, Dougie thought. This was going to be his first real murder mystery: the first case he actually had to solve. Dougie liked the Chief, a solid 16-handicapper who hit the ball reasonably well but suffered from a bit of the whiskey fingers, as the Scots said, around the green. They'd been friends a long time. But Riggs wasn't much younger than Dougie, who'd just semi-retired. The thought of either of them doing anything for the first time at their age was undeniably daunting.

"Morning, Pro!" Dougie heard, and he turned back towards the clubhouse to see his little brother Danny walking towards him with a huge smile splashed across his face. "What a great day!" All of a sudden, Dougie realized again where he was, about to play one of the world's historic golf courses for the first time.

"Morning!" he smiled back at Danny, trying unsuccessfully to put the Judge out of his mind. Maybe there was hope for him and Chief Riggs both, he thought, watching the three mesmerized Bushwood members walk out of the clubhouse and nervously follow Danny down to the practice area.

Two: Bison
Eighteenth Tee
Cypresswood Golf Club – Tradition Course
Spring, Texas

It wasn't like Bison had never won a golf tournament before. He remembered them all. Big Poppa still had a lot of his trophies. His first time was in fifth grade: the Junior Ambassador Classic at River's Edge in North Platte. He won the Arizona state high school tournament and a scholarship to SMU, where he won the Goodwin Intercollegiate on the demanding Stanford University course. He won twice on what was then the Nationwide Tour, at Le Triomphe in Lousiana and Midland CC in West Texas. He even won on the PGA Tour once. It was eight years ago now, at TPC Summerlin in Las Vegas. He made a twenty-five foot birdie putt on the first playoff hole, the long par 4 eighteenth. One of the guys he beat, Charles Howell III, was a two-time winner on tour and a former world top-twenty player.

He'd thought that was it; he thought he'd broken through. Thought he'd just keep winning; thought he belonged. But he hadn't won a single thing since. He lost his tour card just a year later, finishing 152nd on the money list with thirteen missed cuts and no top tens. Closest he'd come to winning again was three years ago. He three-putted the eighteenth to fall out of a four-way playoff at the Cox Classic, the Nationwide—or maybe Web.com by then—event at Champions Run in Omaha. That would have been almost as big for him as Las Vegas, to win in Nebraska. Big Poppa moved them to Phoenix after Mom divorced him, but Bison still felt a connection to his Nebraska birthplace.

He finished top five in a couple of Web.com events last year, but always by coming from behind on Sundays. Sometimes it's easier to score well when you know you can't win. Greg Norman made millions of dollars that way, moving from T38 to T13 by posting a low number in the final round. Bison didn't have any problem with that. He needed the money. But it wasn't the same. It wasn't like being in the hunt.

Now here he was, and unless he went full van de Velde and totally butchered the eighteenth, he was about to win this tournament. It felt pretty good. OK, Bison admitted to himself, maybe, technically, it wasn't really an actual, official win. It was the Monday qualifier for the Houston Open. The low four scores would advance to play in the tournament the rest of the week. He wouldn't get anything more for finishing first than the person who survived the inevitable playoff and secured the final spot. He wouldn't lose anything if Bill Britton, the popular college coach and occasional Champions Tour player he was paired with, somehow picked up three shots on eighteen and beat him by one. But he was two shots ahead of Britton, who was two shots clear of the field, and Bison liked his chances. He was going to shoot a lower score than anyone else. Wasn't that the definition of winning?

He looked down the fairway at the group in front of them waiting. At least one of them was going to take on the lake to the left and have a go at this green. He was pretty sure neither he nor Britton would be having any part of that. Three easy shots, two simple putts, be sure to sign the card right. Bison already had his three wood out. He glanced over and saw that Britton did too.

The eighteenth was a relatively simple par 5, playing 562 yards today. A creek jutted across the fairway about 450 yards from the tee. The hole was guarded by a lake extending up the left side of the kidney-shaped green and two shallow bunkers on the right. It was not one of the more challenging holes on the Tradition course, which was not particularly difficult. As the group in front of them played their second shots, it occurred to Bison that this hole was only about 50 yards longer than the eighteenth at the Golf Club of Houston course he'd be playing the rest of the week. But that was a par 4, and the lake was a lot tighter to the green, and the bunkers were a lot deeper, and the greens were a lot faster and more undulating. Brison smiled with anticipation and reminded himself to focus in the present moment. All he could control right now was putting a solid swing on his three wood.

Britton was up after birdying the short par 4 seventeenth. Bison watched closely as the diminutive shotmaker from Staten Island gathered himself, moved rhythmically through his routine, executed his simple swing, and stroked yet another deadly accurate ball down the middle of the fairway. Under six feet tall and short of 180 pounds, Britton simply didn't have the power and length to compete regularly, even on the Champions Tour, at this stage of his career. But to anyone who knew golf, his swing was still absolutely gorgeous.

"'Nother beautiful shot Bill," Bison said politely. Britton smiled back and handed the club to his caddie, his granddaughter Noel, who stuffed it in their bag with great glee. While they were waiting for the green to clear at the long par 3 eleventh, Britton told Bison he was in Houston visiting his daughter and had entered the qualifier on a whim, in large part so Noel, a promising junior golfer, could caddie for him. Bison suspected her swing was just as beautiful as her granddad's.

Bison, who stood 6'4" and struggled to stay under 270, couldn't remember the last time anyone called his swing beautiful. Powerful, that was the word people used, at least when they were being nice. It bothered him more than he ever let on. He'd never had a real teacher growing up, just Big Poppa. He'd learned the game the way Ben Hogan and Lee Trevino did, beating old balls on dusty ranges under hot sun until his blisters turned to calluses. People liked to say golf was one of those things where if you didn't look good doing it, you probably weren't. But by that measure, either Trevino or Ray Floyd must have been horrible, because their swings were complete opposites, and Bill Britton with his classic swing was surely much, much better than either of them.

So Bison knew that wasn't always how it worked. But he wasn't as driven, as hard-boiled, or as full of himself as Trevino or Floyd either. And they'd played in a different era, when lots of players won with unconventional swings. Now everything was Trackman-optimized and almost without exception all the best players were good little kids from nice neighborhoods who grew up learning the same Tiger Woods-Adam Scott swing from the same coaches and teachers.

Bison stood at the back of the tee and focused in the present, swinging his three wood back and forth idly. Stepping into his stance, he flowed back and through, whipping the club around the full arc of his yoke. He made solid contact and looked up to see his ball heading straight down the middle, about forty yards past Britton's drive. "Oh, that's very nice!" Britton said. "That's going to work great for you at GCH this week!" The atmosphere wasn't quite as competitive as it would be on the 72nd hole of a regular tournament. Then again, Britton was such a nice guy, maybe he'd act the exact same way regardless.

Bison handed his three wood to Hamilton, the quiet bespectacled teenager Big Poppa had found to caddie in the qualifier. Hamilton hadn't spoken to anyone all day except for first tee introductions and a few short exchanges with

Noel about pins and bunker rakes and so on. Noel was charming and beautiful and around his age, so Bison would have understood if Hamilton had been thrown off his game or diverted his attention. But the kid stayed focused. Bison hadn't asked him for any yardages or help reading greens, but he hadn't ever been distracted by him either. After they finished, he and Hamilton would have to talk about the rest of the week. But right now, Bison couldn't think of any reason not to stick with Hamilton. It wasn't like a bunch of tour caddies were going to dump their players, rush over, and chat him up just because he won a Monday qualifier.

Bison followed Hamilton down the tee towards the fairway. He took a look at the small gallery following their group—Noel had more family and fans than the players—but didn't see Big Poppa. He'd been at the course all day, coming and going, wandering back and forwards, periodically bringing scoring reports to augment the patchwork electronic scoring. At GCH, there'd be boards every hole or two. Here, there were just a few. It wasn't always crystal clear who stood where. Big Poppa's updates actually helped.

Big Poppa was there on the eleventh tee when Bison nearly holed a two iron, leaving himself a six-inch tap-in that was worth about a shot-and-a-half on the field. He was with them on the seventh green when Bison curled in a thirty-five foot downhill twister for an unexpected eagle. But he wasn't there on fifteen to watch Bison three-putt from seventeen feet, and he wasn't here now to see him finish.

It wasn't like Big Poppa had never disappeared on him before. Bison was hard pressed to remember the last event Big Poppa came out and watched him play. Big Poppa hadn't been at Las Vegas. Of course—Pebble Beach. Big Poppa wouldn't miss that. Bison had only played there once. He partnered Scott somebody-or-other, a New York businessman who muttered around twenty words and finished about nine holes before they missed the cut by ten. Bison had a vivid memory of Big Poppa dancing around the bar at Spanish Bay. He'd learned at an early age his dad wasn't like other fathers.

He'd never really had a regular job, for one thing. Big Poppa's life hadn't run in a straight line. It was more like an extended cavalcade of schemes and dreams that never quite panned out. Every time his latest plan turned sour, Big Poppa went through a period of remorse and contrition, making extended and heartfelt promises to everyone involved that it would never happen again, right up until it did. His only real loves were his family, fishing, and golf: not necessarily in that order.

Bison's mom finally wised up and filed for divorce the summer before he started high school. Big Poppa shocked everyone by getting custody of the kids. Mom, understandably, flipped out. She moved as far away from North Platte as she could, all the way to Fort Lauderdale.

That's where she met Gene, a retired air traffic controller from Cincinnati. They died in a plane crash over Puerto Rico that Christmas. It was the only time Bison ever saw Big Poppa cry.

They moved to Phoenix that spring so Big Poppa could open a shop selling water filtration systems, which were just cheap charcoal tablets in fancy wrapping paper. That didn't even make it through the summer. Next, Big Poppa started diving for golf balls in water hazards around Arizona. He kept saying he was going to open his own driving range, so Bison and his sister would have someplace to practice, but all he ever did was fill up their trailer with boxes and boxes of worthless old waterlogged golf balls.

Bison's junior year, Big Poppa opened 'Big Poppa's Trophy Dogs,' a glorified hot dog stand featuring exotic meats like kangaroo, alligator, and, of course, bison. That didn't last long because, in true Big Poppa fashion, all his sausages were made out of the same low-grade chicken meat with different seasoning combinations. "Everyone says they all taste like chicken anyway," Big Poppa repeated over and over until he went broke and had to close shop.

After Bison left Arizona and started college in Dallas, he grew less and less inclined to track Big Poppa's entrepreneurial endeavors. He knew there were forays into internet porn production, underground poker rooms, CBD hemp oil ointment, restoring classic cars, and various other schemes promising quick returns on small investments. None of them ever worked out, but Big Poppa stayed out of jail and, as far as Bison knew, he was never homeless.

After Bison won in Las Vegas, he was a little surprised Big Poppa never asked to caddie for him, or manage him, or get into his wallet some other way. It was more success in a week than Big Poppa had managed in his whole lifetime. It might have intimidated him a little. Big Poppa never once asked Bison for money though, no matter how broke he was. That had always meant a lot to Bison.

When he showed up on the door of Bison's apartment in Dallas last week, Big Poppa was bursting at the seams to get to Houston. It was never hard to tell when Big Poppa had money, and this time he was flush. He drove them down in a new Land Rover. He set them up with adjoining balcony suites up the road at the Woodlands Resort. Big Poppa diligently shuttled Bison back and forth to Cypresswood, wearing a tasteful new golf outfit every day. He took Bison across town to Ray's BBQ Shack for fall-off-the-bone ribs, fried catfish, the best fried corn-on-the-cob he'd ever had, and something called dirty rice. It was a great week. Bison was starting to enjoy having Big Poppa around.

Britton hit his second shot, another fairway wood, safely short of the creek but well within wedge range. Bison thought for a moment about hitting a short iron. He had just under 200 yards to cover the creek, about 70 yards of fairway past that, and 110 yards total from the creek to the green. There were two or three clubs he could hit over the creek to leave himself an easy half-wedge. He looked over and saw Britton laughing with Noel. He decided that right next to Britton, short of the creek, was where he wanted to be.

Hamilton nodded when Bison pulled his eight iron, which set him back a moment. It was the most feedback the teenager had given him all day. He wasn't even sure the kid knew the first thing about golf. He stepped back and made a few loose practice swipes. "Play conservative, swing aggressive," he thought to himself. Focusing in the moment, he stepped into his stance and whipped the club around his yoke to Britton's ball.

He missed short and right by a few feet, but that was fine. Hamilton nodded again when Bison handed him the eight iron. Bison thought about saying something, but decided to wait until after the round. He was going to have to have a talk with the kid anyway. They continued up the fairway, watching Britton and Noel smile and laugh as their family and friends congratulated them.

As they approached their balls, Bison saw Big Poppa walking back towards them from the green. As usual, he looked like a fisherman. His khaki vest had a black collar and four pockets. His bucket hat didn't have anything stuck in it, just a few stained reminders of lures he'd lost.

Bison had to give him credit though. His brand new golf slacks, polo shirt, and plain black sneakers were clean and unobtrusive. Big Poppa had definitely toned things down. Not once had he gone full Arizona pastel, or worn jeans, or done anything else to stick out from the crowd. It wasn't like him.

Big Poppa was still leaning on his big silver cane. He'd never known Big Poppa to have any hip or leg issues, and it wasn't something they'd ever talked about before, but he'd been using it constantly ever since he showed up. He seemed to get in and out of cars OK, though, and he was typically vague about what exactly was wrong with him, what doctor was treating him, what the prognosis was, and things like that. Bison figured maybe he was so used to having a fishing rod or a golf club in his hand that he just needed something to hold on to in order to feel comfortable. His cane certainly wasn't holding Big Poppa back as he marched down the fairway towards them.

The green cleared ahead of them and Bison prepared to play his wedge shot from 130 to the center of the green. Focusing in the moment, he whipped around his yoke right on target, leaving himself a simple uphill twenty-five foot birdie putt. He heard Big Poppa yell and looked over to see him shaking his cane in the air from the side of the fairway. Bison smiled and waved at him.

Britton had displayed a beautiful mastery from this distance all day. Even though he had nothing more to gain than Bison, if much less to lose, it must have been difficult for such an artiste to play away from the pin from here. He fired a beauty that landed softly and curled confidently to rest no more than five feet from the hole. Noel clapped enthusiastically and hopped up and down in glee as a polite cheer went through the Britton family gallery. Bison would have bet everything he had, right there, that Noel would get ten times as much TV time this week caddying as he would playing. He had no problem with that. The entire Britton family was adorable.

They all started moving towards the hole. Bison smiled at Big Poppa again. Maybe their family wasn't that adorable, but Bison was glad Big Poppa was here. Maybe, just maybe, their best times were still ahead of them. Bison lagged back and let the Brittons approach the green first, waving their hats to acknowledge the cheers of their gallery and the other players around the green.

Hamilton set the bag down next to Big Poppa, walked over, and handed Bison his putter. Apropos of nothing, Bison wondered for a moment whether Hamilton would take the flag home with him, as winning caddies traditionally did. Then Bison realized that the other players around the green were not watching because they found the Britton family adorable. They were waiting for the playoff for the final qualifying spot, or spots, which was going to start on this hole after they and the group behind them finished. He shook his head and tried to bring himself back into the present long enough to make two simple putts.

He walked around his putt but didn't see much. Bison thought for a second about asking Hamilton for a read, just to see what the kid would do, but decided against it. Things were going so great. He'd played so well. Big Poppa was on his best behavior. Shut up and keep your head down, he told himself. Don't borrow trouble.

Focusing in the moment, he connected to the path and stroked around his yoke back and through to the hole. His ball wiggled slightly left and right but held true and dropped neatly into the center of the cup at a perfect pace. Bison smiled and lifted his putter into the air. What a way to finish! Maybe this was the week his career turned around!

He tipped his cap to the greenside gallery, acknowledging their polite applause, and walked up to retrieve his ball. "That's a beautiful rhythm," Britton told him. "You're going to putt great this week!" "Thanks Bill," Bison acknowledged. "It's really helped me, watching you today. Knock this in!" Bison pulled his ball from the hole and handed his putter to Hamilton, who was grinning from ear to ear. "Good job!" Bison told him. The kid just nodded and grinned even more.

Britton went through his normal routine, but Bison knew there wasn't much chance of him missing the short putt under these circumstances. Sure enough, the old pro put it right in the center of the cup, eliciting another shriek from Noel. She ran up and jumped into her grandfather's arms like they'd just won the U.S. Open. Britton's smile, Bison thought, spoke of something even more valuable.

He walked up and politely shook hands with Bill and Noel, who was hopping up and down again. A couple of the other players came over and congratulated him. He thanked them and wished the playoff participants well. Finally, the green began to clear—there'd be no trophy or ceremony, just a single-page entry form for them to fill out—and Bison made his way over to the side of the fairway next to his bag, where Big Poppa was standing. His face was beaming every bit as much as Noel's.

"Well old man," Bison smiled, "I guess you're gonna have to stick around here for the rest of the week. Hope you didn't have any plans!?"

Big Poppa laughed and looked around the green. He rested his cane on Bison's bag. He looked down briefly. Then he reached up, took Bison's face between his hands like Payne Stewart at the U.S. Open, and looked straight into his eyes. "You're going to win the Masters!!!!"

Three: Danny
First Tee
Augusta National Golf Club
Augusta, Georgia

Danny was pissed. Fuming mad, pacing around the back of the first tee, grumbling at his world. This, he had to admit with a rue smile, was certainly not how he'd ever pictured the start of his first round at Augusta National.

His day started so well. He woke up even earlier than he expected. He was full of excitement and unable to contain himself. He ate a classic southern breakfast at a local diner on Washington Road, breaking into giggles every few minutes thinking about what they were about to do. He arrived at the course just as the gates opened, more than two hours before their first tee time. He took advantage of the early morning quiet and enjoyed a long hot shower in the members' locker room. It was amazing. Danny had been in a lot of memorable showers in his life, but none that came close to that. Probably after that he should have just walked back down Magnolia Lane and found his way home without even talking to Dougie and the rest of them.

He took his time in the empty locker room. Danny carefully redonned the outfit he'd planned on wearing his first round here ever since he was twelve years old and won the intermediate boys flight of the Nebraska Golf Association Junior Championship with rounds of 74 and 76 at Norfolk Country Club. Solid black shoes with black laces. Medium-gray, medium-wide, flat-front slacks. A plain black belt. And an old-school short-sleeve, white golf shirt with all three buttons fastened, no logos, and sharp points on the broad collars.

Except for Danny's white Nike hat, it was more or less the exact outfit Hogan wore in 1953 when he broke the scoring record by five strokes and won the tournament by the same margin after posting four straight rounds in the 60's. It was more or less what Snead wore on Monday in 1954 when he bested Hogan by a single stroke after posting three birdies on the back nine in their historic playoff. It's what Arnie wore in 1964 when the King won his last major by six over Jack. And, even though Danny sometimes had trouble believing it, Dad swore to him that, except for the shoes, it was exactly what the Wardrobe himself, Jimmy Demaret, wore in 1950 when he became the first ever three-time Masters Champion.

Hogan, Snead, the King, and the Wardrobe. Those were Danny's father's heroes. They'd become Danny's first golf heroes. Dad never doubted for a moment Danny would play here someday, but he'd dammed sure never imagined it would be from the members tees with these two jackass lawyers. Danny glanced over at the two fat white men squawking and pointing fingers at each other. He turned and looked back up past the clubhouse towards the morning sun and Magnolia Lane, wondering again if he should just walk away.

Danny had been more than a little unsure about this trip from the very beginning, even before he found out Judge Smails was dead. He loved his big brother, and he knew Dougie loved him, but they didn't spend much time together. They certainly never talked much about some of the elephants that followed them around.

Dougie spent his whole life in North Platte married to one wonderful woman, Heidi, working at one horrible place, Bushwood, and raising three amazing daughters. Danny left North Platte for good just a few weeks after he graduated from high school. He hadn't gotten a paycheck in at least thirty years and he had a long history of questionable decisions with evanescent women. He hadn't married any of them, and he'd never been a father.

They'd both lived rich, interesting lives in very different ways. It didn't give them a lot of common ground, not to mention everything that happened with Mom, and then with Dad passing away. So Danny had been more than a little surprised last December when he'd heard the voicemail from Minnie, the Bushwood club secretary, inviting him on Dougie's retirement trip. Nobody had ever offered Danny a trip to Augusta National before. It was a damn hard thing for any golfer to turn down.

Dougie and his members took three-stop coach flights from North Platte to Augusta via Denver and Atlanta, arriving late last night. Danny cashed the Bushwood check

Minnie sent him and used some Delta miles to fly first-class to Atlanta yesterday. He rented a Range Rover and made the short drive over to Augusta.

When he'd called Minnie back, she'd invited Danny to stay with Dougie and the others at "Mr. Kellerman's vacation home," but the thought made him queasy. Instead, he'd booked a suite at one of the corporate hotels clustered around the freeway east of the course itself, which was famously surrounded by low rent strip malls. He'd used their late arrival as a convenient excuse for not seeing the others until this morning, so he hadn't learned they were one Judge short until he caught up with Dougie on the driving range about forty minutes ago.

It had been awkward. Dougie, who was usually so composed and stoic, was clearly upset when Danny walked down the hill and saw him standing alone on the range. Danny called out to him with all the grace his voice could muster, forgoing any of his usual sarcasm. Instead of a polite handshake, they fell into a deep embrace for the first time in years. Maybe, Danny thought, for the first time since Dad's funeral.

"He's dead," Danny heard his brother's soft voice say. He felt Dougie trembling in his arms. "Judge Smails. He's dead."

"What!?" Danny pulled back.

"It's true," Dougie nodded. "He's dead."

Danny stared mutely at his brother. His mind flashed

back to the last time he'd seen Judge Smails, at the Nebraska State High School Championships. It was at Bushwood, his senior year. He'd won by five shots after casually three-putting the last two greens for bogies without really lining up or thinking much about any of his putts. That, he'd figured, was the point of having a seven-shot lead with two to play.

The Judge hadn't seen it that way. He'd been outraged. He stormed out onto the eighteenth green and made a scene. He screamed at Danny, at Dad, at poor Coach Sportesto, and at everyone else within earshot. "A disgrace! A disgrace to the game!" That's what Danny remembered the most. The Judge, who cheated constantly and still couldn't break 90, was livid Danny hadn't "given it his all" to finish eight or nine under instead of "just" seven under. That, the Judge proclaimed, was "unforgivable!"

And, Danny had to admit, the Judge probably never did forgive him, not that he'd ever given two shits what that self-righteous hypocrite thought. "Some people can't face themselves," Dad told him that night, "so they spend their lives blustering at others."

Dad sure called that one right. Danny remembered the first time he'd crossed paths with Smails, way back before he got appointed Judge. Danny was just eight or nine. Dougie had just started working in the Bushwood pro shop full-time, after years in the bag room. Dougie talked

him into coming out and caddying one weekend. Danny
got the bag of a guest, Richard, who was a pretty good
player. On the par 4 twelfth, where players walked back up
to the elevated tee, Richard took his driver and sent Danny
down to the landing area, confident his drive would find the
fairway.

As Danny walked down the edge of the rough, he
watched the group behind them approach the eleventh
green. A small skittish man in a pink shirt around Dougie's
age walked quickly out ahead of his group and caught
Danny's eye. Danny watched him walk up on the green
and mark his ball, leaning on his putter to support himself.
He walked back around the green, laughing loudly, while
Richard and the rest of Danny's group drove down into the
twelfth fairway. Danny saw them start down from the tee
and idly looked back at the eleventh green.

The man in the pink shirt was ready to putt. But,
Danny saw immediately, he wasn't putting from where his
ball landed! He was putting from six or seven feet closer to
the hole! The angle from Danny's position in the twelfth
fairway made it obvious. Danny kept staring. He putted
and missed. The short-hitters in Danny's group came to
their drives. Danny hustled to beat Richard to his ball.

Richard wedged onto the twelfth green and Danny
looked back at the eleventh green in time to see the man in
the pink shirt sweep his ball away and walk off the green
after his second putt was conceded. Danny darted up to

read Richard's birdie putt and tried to forget about the whole thing.

But after Richard and the rest of Danny's group holed out on eighteen, Danny stood by the side of the green and watched the other group finish. This time, he noticed, one of the other players, a red-haired man with green pants and a white belt, got to the green first. The man in the pink shirt didn't bother marking his ball, which was barely on the front edge of the green. His approach putt came up about four feet short and he swatted his ball across the green towards his caddie, telling the rest of his group "that's enough for me today." Danny cleaned Richard's clubs, thanked him, and rode his bike home.

That evening he and Dad were hitting chip shots to each other in the backyard. Danny told him about seeing the man in the pink shirt putt closer to the hole on the eleventh, and how he swatted his ball off the eighteenth green. "Did he mark his ball on eleven like this?" Dad asked, leaning on his club as he reached down behind his ball and picked it up.

"Yes!" Danny said.

"That's an old one!" Dad nodded. "Look." Dad licked a plastic ball marker and quickly reached down and stuck it to the bottom of his sand wedge. Then he bent down and pretended to put a marker down behind his ball while he leaned on the wedge that stuck out in front of him. "Then you walk around the green," Dad demonstrated, "so people forget where you were, and when you walk back …" he was five or six feet closer, just like the man in the pink shirt.

Danny was shocked. He'd seen kids cheat before, but only in blatant and unsophisticated ways: denying shots had ever occurred; intentionally miscounting; not taking obvious penalties. This was subtler and, somehow, more treacherous. You had to plan ahead to cheat like that.

Later, when Dougie came home, Danny couldn't wait to tell him what he'd seen. To his amazement, Dougie denied everything. "Elihu wouldn't do that!" he'd insisted. "You must have moved—your angle changed. It's a long way from the eleventh green to the landing area on twelve. There's no way you could be sure."

"I know what I saw!" Danny insisted. But Dougie hammered away at the distance and the angle, and how far behind their group Smails was, and how Danny was holding Richard's bag, and a bunch of other things that didn't seem relevant to Danny.

They'd argued long enough to annoy Dad, who promptly quashed their dispute. "Only thing to do about a cheater is not play them again," he'd told them. "Since neither one of you was playing him, it isn't your problem right now, is it?"

They'd both nodded and stopped squabbling, but it was too late. The damage was done. Danny never caddied again. They started playing less and less golf together.

Dougie could only ever have one guest at Bushwood, every other Monday after 2:00, even after he became the head pro. He could never play with both Dad and Danny, so he wound up rarely inviting either of them.

By the time he turned eleven, Danny was regularly threatening par at River's Edge. Like any precocious junior who wasn't a complete jerk, he quickly became a favorite of the pro, Dick Churchman, and many of the regulars. Dick and Dad were old friends, so Danny and Dad spent more and more time at River's Edge, while Dougie mostly played with the members at Bushwood, and their golf just drifted further and further apart. Then Mom died and Danny left North Platte and everything blew apart. Then Dad died. They hadn't talked much since his funeral.

"I'm sorry about the Judge." Danny told his brother. "I can't believe you're here! I can't believe you still came. I can't believe anyone came. Well, I can believe it …." He waved his arm towards the par three course. It was the most beautiful piece of land he'd ever seen.

"But," Dougie nodded. "But, you aren't sure you should believe it … But, maybe you don't want to believe it. I know. I went through a lot of those ifs and buts last night myself."

"You OK," he asked?

"Yeah," Dougie assured him. "Maybe. I don't know." Dougie was holding a long iron. There was a confused look on his face. "It's been a hard couple of days."

"What happened?" Danny asked. He was terrified Smails died at Bushwood and Dougie had to watch him pass. It was, Dad told him many times, one of the worst things about the golf business: so many of the customers wanted so badly to die on the premises when their time came.

"Somebody killed him," Dougie said quietly. "Shoved a shower rod down his throat."

Danny didn't know what to say. Smails was a despicable scumbag, but murder? In North Platte? He couldn't remember anyone ever being murdered in North Platte. "I'm so sorry," was all he could tell his brother. Dougie nodded. He half-heartedly knocked a three-quarter long iron down the middle of the range. "Jesus! Are you sure you want to do this?" Danny asked. Dougie smacked another ball down the middle, a little harder this time.

"Yeah," Dougie nodded. "I mean …" and he waved his arm at Magnolia Drive off to the left of the range and back towards Ike's Pond on the other side.

"OK then," Danny told him, "if we're going to do this, let's do it! Let's make some birdies! Heck, it's not like we don't know the course! Let's focus, relax, visualize, and execute the shit out of this motherfucker!"

Dougie smiled. "OK," he nodded. "Let's do it! But we can't play together, at least not today. The Judge's friend Postlewaite, he told me we have to put a member in each group. So we have to split up him and the other member, Kellerman. Two of the Bushwood guys made me promise I'd play the first round with them. Bill Turin, everyone calls him Chompers, and Pork Chop, Phil McDonald. I think they're pretty nervous. Heck, I'm pretty nervous! But we'll play together tomorrow for sure!"

That was bad enough, to have to play Augusta National with strangers and not with Dougie. But then they left the driving range and walked up the hill past the clubhouse and the famous tree to the putting green and the first tee. The Judge's friends were waiting for them.

It wasn't just that they were rich, old, white assholes, Danny thought, watching Postlewaite gesture emphatically at Stewart Cottleston, the Bushwood member in their threesome. They couldn't help that. Stewie, as he'd introduced himself to Danny, was poking his finger right back at Smiley, jabbering away, his eyes locked on their host. Dougie said the guys at Bushwood called him Sterno because of his quick temper.

It was how totally self-centered and self-absorbed they all were. These two lawyers had only just met but had no problem going at each other like an old married couple right here on the first tee of Augusta National. They didn't care one whit how ugly they looked to those they considered beneath them, like Danny and the caddies. "Of course it's about the money," Danny heard Stewie say as he turned away from their host and walked back to his bag, like that was the end of their conversation.

"About whose money?" Postlewaite shot back, but Stewie ignored him. Generally Danny didn't play golf with people for money. But he thought for a moment about the prospect of a "friendly little game" with these two puffed shirts. Watching them shoot mental daggers at each other, he decided to stick with his policy. Better to avoid both of them as much as possible. Beating them might sound good now, but in the end it would undoubtedly be awkward and intense and, even if they played for chump change, he'd probably never get paid anyway. Plus, he'd have to talk to them. It was hard to imagine any of them ever talking about anything but themselves.

They'd set that tone right from the start. "I'm Charlie Kellerman," the smaller, wirier one pronounced as they'd approached the first tee. "This is Miles Postlewaite."

"Call me Smiley," Postlewaite interjected with a forced smile, looking like he'd rather be just about anywhere than on the first tee of one of the two most famous golf courses in the world on a beautiful spring morning. "He's Chucky!"

"I'll be playing in the first group with the pro and two of the Bushwood members," Kellerman continued. "The younger brother and the other Bushwood member will follow with Miles. We'll pick up anything over double bogey. Our groups will finish in no more than three hours and fifty minutes. There are three other groups on the course right now. If we catch up with any of them, we'll stay exactly one hole behind. There will be at least twenty more groups behind us. It would be unfortunate, as we say here at the National, if we delayed any of them."

It was not the least friendly starter speech Danny had ever heard. But it certainly wasn't very welcoming. Chucky couldn't make it any clearer he was just doing this because he had to, that he wasn't at all interested in getting to know any of them. He didn't mention the Judge at all. Danny wondered again why Chucky and Smiley hadn't just called this whole thing off.

And if they were going to hold anyone up, it sure looked like Chucky would be the reason why. He'd taken the honor in the first group as a matter of right, without saying anything to anyone, including his caddie. His pre-shot routine was complex and hard to describe. He started with his driver pointed behind him. Then, after some forced breathing and deep knee bends, Chucky gradually wiggled himself into place over the ball. Two slow rehearsal moves later, he finally pulled the club back violently and slashed down with all his might, producing a weak carp that came to rest about 185 yards down the right side of the fairway. He picked up his tee, looking pleased with himself.

Danny tried to think of ways to avoid watching that all morning. He glanced at Chompers and Pork Chop and saw hints of smiles. Their faces were a lot looser. They knew they could beat that swing like a rug. All of a sudden, they were a little less nervous about being here, not quite as intimidated by the Judge's big city law school buddies, maybe even a bit less overwhelmed by the Judge's death.

Dougie, with a respectful nod from Pork Chop, stepped up next. Danny felt a wave of pride wash through him at the sight of his big brother on the first tee at Augusta. Dougie was a senior, so playing these tees was no big deal for him. Danny smiled as he watched Dougie flow through his pre-shot routine.

His brother had never been a great player. He worked hard to stay competitive with other senior club pros. His swing was much more mechanical than Danny's had ever been, or could ever be. Dougie had always spent a lot more time at the range and on the practice green than Danny ever did, or ever could. But Dougie's swing was fundamentally sound and Danny knew his routine by heart. He proudly watched him focus, relax, visualize and execute a solid three wood with a slight fade to the middle of the fairway, about 140 yards out. "Nice shot. pro," Danny quietly offered, giving his big brother an enthusiastic golf clap. Dougie smiled at him and raised his club in the air before handing it to his caddie.

Chompers and Pork Chop hit controlled fades with drivers into the general vicinity of Dougie's three wood. Their flawed but effective techniques established right away how much golf they played. They might not make any birdies, but they probably wouldn't make many double bogies either. Danny looked over at Chucky, wondering if it was as obvious to him who was going to have the high score in that group, but he was lecturing his caddie about the proper arrangement of his clubs, oblivious to his playing partners.

As Dougie's group moved out, Danny shook hands with his caddie, Tobias. Tobias looked him up and down. "First time here with us, right?"

"Yep," Danny smiled. "I'm the little brother."

"You play any golf then, little brother?"

"Little bit, here and there."

"What's the best course you ever played?"

"Royal Melbourne."

"OK," Tobias nodded. "You think you got any idea how to play this hole?" He pointed to the crest of the hill, a little more than 200 yards down the fairway.

"A few," Danny smiled. "How about up there, to start?" He nodded back up the hill towards the tournament tees.

"OK, I see how it is." Tobias looked him up and down again. "Alright, how you play it from back there then?"

"Driver," Danny replied, "down the middle. Middle of the green. Two putt, maybe make one. Move on. Don't take any chances. No shame in bogey on the first."

Tobias nodded. "Good. That's how you play it from

there alright. OK, now: since there ain't no chance in hell they going to let you play it back there, what're you gonna do from here?"

Danny looked down the hill at the fairway. In his disappointment at not playing with Dougie from the real tee he'd imagined his whole life, he hadn't really given any thought to how to play from here. "Same thing, I guess," he told Tobias. "Hit it where Dougie did, right at the top of the hill, maybe a little further. About 130 out. Hit it on the middle of the green, two putt, move on."

Tobias shook his head. "Nope." He pulled Danny's driver from the bag and pointed at the bunker on the right. "Not even close. You even half as good as you think you are, you take this and you pure it over the very left edge of that bunker. It will roll down to the bottom of the hill, leave us a little wedge. From that tee," he pointed back up the hill, "par is a great number, like you said. From here," he pointed down at the ground, "it's less than 220 to cover that bunker. It's a completely different hole. You hit it to the bottom of the hill, you hit a soft little wedge, we make birdie. You can't do that, you got no reason to want any part of this whole course. You seem to think you do, so let's see what you got, right here!"

Danny nodded. Maybe this was going to work out after all. Things usually did. Mercifully, Smiley's pre-shot routine and swing were relatively normal. He had a short, controlled backswing that sacrificed distance for accuracy.

It served him well in this case. He hit a low straight driver that rolled out just about even with Dougie's three wood.

Stewie was just the opposite. He 'got his money's worth,' they probably said around the bar at Bushwood, coming up on both toes and audibly grunting as he lashed as hard as he could at the ball. He easily carried the hill but went in the woods far to the left. Danny figured it probably wouldn't be the last time he visited the famed Augusta pines.

Danny stepped up and teed it on the right side of the box to draw it back to the middle. He stood behind the ball and waggled a few times, feeling the energy of this hallowed ground with his feet. When he saw the ball taking the line he wanted over the left edge of the bunker, he relaxed and let the club follow its path. He caught it well and picked up his tee as his drive headed over the corner of the bunker to the middle of the fairway at the bottom of the hill.

"OK little brother," Tobias nodded as he took Danny's driver. "You just keep doing what you're told, we're gonna do just fine out here."

Four: Hope
Fifth Green
Shelter Cove Golf Course by The Sea
Shelter Cove, California

Big Poppa once told her golf exposes people like standing naked in church. At the time, she was a seventeen-year-old high school senior, an all-state shooting guard, and the reigning Miss Arizona. He was a divorced second-rate porn producer who hadn't been to church since his wedding day and was about to get them evicted from their trailer. So she hadn't paid him much mind then, or for quite a few years afterwards.

Hope hadn't always honored and respected her father like she should, but Big Poppa never stopped being part of her life. He barely made it to the church in time for her wedding, but he got there. He hadn't met his only grandchild until her son was three, but he never failed to call on Gabriel's birthday. He never quit and never stopped trying. He'd left her messages from strange places at random times with strained excuses for as long as she could remember.

So last summer, when Gabriel started getting interested in golf and talked her into playing again, Hope naturally thought about Big Poppa. She hadn't played golf since her last high school tournament her senior year. Mostly what she remembered was the long, quiet van ride home, thinking about how to tell Big Poppa she'd shot 86 and cost the Lady Dons an opportunity to play in the state championship. Big Poppa was always so happy when Bison won golf tournaments. She'd always wanted to give him that same joy.

But however disappointed he'd been, Big Poppa handled it well. He just hugged her quietly and told her how proud of her he was. How proud Mom would have been. He'd only asked her to play golf once or twice after that, and hadn't pressured her much when she declined. She'd been relieved. She knew how much golf meant to him.

And he'd taught her well. Hope couldn't deny that hitting good shots was a big part of what made golf so rewarding for her now. When she and Gabriel went out that first time, she'd started hitting crisp, obedient little draws right away. She made her first birdie since high school, right here on number five, the uphill par 3 at the north end of the runway that sat in the middle of the little nine-hole community course nestled between her town and the edge of the Pacific.

After her ball went in the hole, she'd raised her putter in the air and looked around. On a clear summer day like that, the view extended north over the ocean all the way up to Sea Lion Gulch. To the south, she could see the whole cove extending out down towards Abalone Point. Her son stood next to her, beaming with pride. And all around her, from just about every house in town, people could look out their windows and watch them putt. That's when she'd remembered Big Poppa's line about standing naked in church. Now, every time she played this hole, Hope thought about Big Poppa and felt like she was standing naked in front of her whole town. She never felt like that in church.

As soon as she and Gabriel finished that first round last summer, they went straight across the street to Abalone Hall, the community clubhouse, where she bought them a $500 yearly membership. Gabriel hadn't caught the bug like her, at least not yet. They still played together once a month or so, but he wasn't enthralled by the game like Hope was. He had to go to school, and his friends were more into skateboards and video games, so he had less free time and more social options than she did. She'd promised herself long ago that she'd never pressure Gabriel to do anything but be a good person.

Hope played just about every day now, even in the damp winter months. That made her one of the few regulars at Shelter Cove, a course so small and remote there was no pro shop, or Tuesday morning ladies club, or anything like that. But there was Vern's Fairway Mini Mart across the street from the ninth green, which had better tri-tip sandwiches than anything this side of San Francisco, with cold beer and tables where you could sit and talk with your friends about golf, and life, and other important things. When you got down to it, Hope reflected, golf was mostly just an excuse to spend quality time with good people. Mostly, she thought, but maybe not entirely.

"So how did Gabriel's project turn out?" Veeka asked from the other side of the green. "The one about his family history?" Veeka and her husband Peter were two of Hope's new golf friends. They were young parents who came to her church occasionally. She'd never really talked to them until they pulled into the community center parking lot alongside her one afternoon last fall. Now, they talked almost every day. They played with her at least once or twice a week. She liked playing with them because they loved each other so much.

"He's still working on it," Hope replied. "It's hard. It's not like anyone on my side of the family lives here, or returns my calls, or uses social media, or keeps up with each other. He didn't have any trouble with Jason's family of course!" Gabriel's father grew up northeast of Garberville. His family was deeply entrenched in the marijuana industry, which had been the region's main economic engine for the past few generations. It wasn't the Corleone family, but they were insulated and close-knit. Gabriel had more than enough stories and vignettes to share about his father's kinfolk, even if some of them might have to be edited a little first.

"How does that make Gabriel feel?" Peter asked, looking over his birdie putt. He was the best golfer Hope had played with at Shelter Cove. He'd grown up south of Garberville and played this course his whole life with his dad, his grandfather, and soon their three-year-old son Irwin, who was taking a nap in his stroller by the side of the green. One of the nicest things about Shelter Cove was how much people encouraged bringing dogs and children.

"You think I know!" Hope laughed. "I'm just his mother!" Gabriel didn't talk about Big Poppa much. He seemed happy enough to talk when Big Poppa called, but it's not like they'd ever spent much time together. Gabriel had only met Bison twice, when he was just a baby, so it's not like they had any relationship. And that was it. It was just the three of them on her side of Gabriel's family, at least as far as she knew. On Jason's side, of course, it was a whole different ball game. "I know he loves Jason's family," she sighed, "but of course he does! There's so many of them, and they're all so close...."

"And they're all here with him!" Veeka exclaimed. "Around him all the time! I know just what you mean. It's strange, isn't it," she continued, "how you want your children to have a connection to 'your' family—maybe even more of a connection than you want for yourself!—and how that somehow makes you jealous of their 'other' family that's actually here, doing the work, being part of their lives." She watched Peter sink his putt.

"I feel that way about Irwin sometimes," Veeka continued. "Already! He's three! Peter's mom and dad, and his sisters, and the cousins … they're all wonderful! We're so lucky to have them here with us. But sometimes, when I watch Alicia, or anyone—it doesn't have anything to do with her, you know—holding Irwin, I wish *my* brother was holding him. I'm sad my brother isn't holding him, sad he doesn't want to hold Irwin bad enough to come visit us. Then I get jealous and angry at Alicia, because she *is* holding him, and then I realize how stupid that is, and so finally I get frustrated and upset with myself!" She nodded her head at Hope. "Sure, I get it."

Peter picked his ball out of the hole and looked at her. "You never told me that." He glanced over at Irwin. "We've talked about waiting to visit your family until Irwin was old enough to remember it—do you think that's a bad idea?"

"No, no, of course not," Veeka agreed. "That's not what I meant! I was just trying to explain to Hope how it makes me feel."

"I get it," Hope assured her. "Jason's family is amazing. They could not have done more for Gabriel, or for me. My family is not amazing. They haven't done much for us at all. So I wish 'we'—the family *I* came from—were more like 'them'—the family I married into— and it makes me feel frustrated and jealous and confused and mostly I just take it out on myself. I totally get it."

"My family is so much more dysfunctional than Peter's," Veeka mused. "You have no idea. That doesn't mean," she reassured Peter, "that we need to fix them, or to put more effort into seeing them than they put into seeing us. It doesn't mean we have to *do* anything. It just makes me feel like I'm missing something, like I'm failing somehow, and I don't even know why or how."

"Because they're still your family," Hope nodded. "That's it. And you feel like they're bringing you down. It's like, after Gabriel writes all these stories about his adventures with Jason's family—about his Uncle Jake, and his cousins, and Bompa Dave and Bomma Stacie, who've spoiled him rotten his whole life—what else can he say? 'My other grandma died when my mom was just a baby and she doesn't really remember her or know much of anything about her past. My other grandfather is a get-rich-quick schemer who calls on my birthday and Christmas and talks funny to me. I have another uncle I met once or twice when I was a baby.' It's just how things are, but it's hard not to take it personally. It's hard not to feel like it makes *me* look bad."

"Of course it's hard!" Veeka nodded. "Families are hard!"

"So why don't you do something about it?" Peter asked as he replaced the flag and they walked over to the sixth tee.

"Like what?" Hope looked at him. "If you know how I can trade in my family, I'm all ears."

"Not trade in," Peter smiled. "Do something about not knowing more about your mother! Do something about you and Gabriel not having more stories to tell about your family. Heck, didn't you tell us your brother was a golf pro!? Is he still playing? Couldn't you take Gabriel to watch a tournament—I bet he'd like that?"

"Last summer, when Gabriel got you started playing golf again, did you talk about your brother?" Veeka added.

"No, I don't think so," Hope answered. She fell quiet for a second as they teed off on the course's only par 5. As usual, Peter hit a screaming low fade that bounced across the runway tarmac five or six times before scampering back into the fairway more than 300 yards below them. As always, his shot made her smile. It made just about everyone he played with smile. Most people liked to see other people get away with little things like that, cutting the ball back into play off of the forbidden airport pavement. It felt like getting away with something that technically wasn't illegal but probably should have been.

They started down the fairway towards Veeka and Hope's more conventional drives. "I think Bison is still trying to play in tournaments," she said. "I don't think he's done so well, though, these last few years. We don't really talk about it, not that I ever talk to him as it is." She paused for a second. "If he is, I guess I could at least ask Gabriel if going to one of Bison's tournaments sounded interesting."

"Wouldn't it be fun to go to a pro tournament?" Peter shook his head. "Or maybe it would just be disappointing, seeing in person exactly how much better they are."

"But she wouldn't just be there to watch," Veeka

pointed out. "She'd be there to root for her brother! To help him win!"

Hope laughed. "It's been a long time since I watched Bison play golf, but unless he's really changed, I doubt he'd even notice we were there." She waited while Veeka hit her second shot. "It's not like basketball. Fans don't have any effect on the game."

"Maybe that's something Gabriel would be interested in," Peter replied, "seeing how focused Bison and the rest of the players are on their golf. That sort of focus, that professionalism, that's a good lesson for anyone! Maybe that would turn into a good family story for him."

"Maybe," Hope admitted. "In a way I hope he thinks they're all just weird."

"What do you mean?"

Hope hit a five iron down the middle of the fairway. "It's hard to explain," she started. "But, and again, it's been a long time, but when I remember Bison playing golf, I don't remember a lot of joy." She put her club back in her bag and looked over at Peter. He was smiling, one hand wrapped in his wife's and the other resting on his son's stroller. "I don't remember him having fun like we do. I don't remember him being happy."

"But I thought you said he's really good?" Veeka asked. "Wouldn't that be fun?"

"Maybe," Hope replied. "I don't know! It was a long time ago. I mean, I was really young! I didn't know anything. And I've never really talked to him very much about his tournaments—we don't talk much at all these days. But I'll never forget it. I would have been just eight or nine, when he won the state high school tournament. In Arizona. I remember feeling like it never really made him happy at all. It didn't seem to bring him any joy. It was more like he was just relieved he hadn't lost. I don't want Gabriel to start feeling like that. I just want him to have fun and be happy."

Peter nodded. "I can see that. I was never that good, not even close to it. Growing up, though, I played with a couple of guys like that, who were really good. Sometimes it seemed like all they cared about was not losing, not messing up. Like they were playing to avoid fear, not to find joy." He looked at Hope. "I think a lot of them were scared of disappointing their fathers, letting them down. Do you think your dad might have had anything to do with it?"

"I don't know." Hope thought about it for a second. "Maybe. Maybe not. I remember once I was scared that I'd let him down. I played really bad in my last high school golf match. He handled it great though. But he was so much more intense about Bison's golf, I remember that too. I don't know. I was just so young!"

"Do your dad and brother get along now?" Veeka asked. "If you and Gabriel did go visit them, would you want to visit them both at once, or which one would you want to visit first?"

"Ooh, good question!" Hope thought for a moment. "I think maybe just Bison first. Like you said, at a golf tournament. At least we'll know he'll be there!" She chuckled and watched Veeka hit her iron shot to the green. "Maybe he'll play a tournament that's somewhere touristy, like New Orleans or Nashville, and we can have a vacation *and* a visit."

"What about your mom? How could you and Gabriel learn more about her? Do you know if she or your dad had any other relatives?"

"I don't know," Hope admitted as they walked down the edge of the runway towards Peter's drive. "Mom died in a plane crash, over Puerto Rico, when I was just a little girl. After she divorced my dad. I was only five I think. I just don't remember any other relatives growing up, ever."

"Oh my gosh," Veeka cried. "I'm so sorry about your Mom! How tragic."

"Horrible!" Peter added. "What a miserable thing for a little girl to have to go through."

"Thanks," Hope assured them. "I was so young, though. I didn't really understand anything. I don't think I ever saw Mom again, after the divorce. She moved away. Somewhere in Florida I think."

"From Phoenix?"

"No, from North Platte, in Nebraska. That's where I was born," Hope told them. "I think Mom was born there too. We moved to Phoenix right after she died. I haven't been back to Nebraska since then."

"Wait," Peter hesitated, "I don't want to ask any uncomfortable questions, but are you saying she moved to Florida without you? Do you know why she would do that?"

"Peter!" Veeka interrupted.

"No," Hope assured them, "it's OK! That's … that's a good question! I never really thought about it. I've never sat down and gone over the timing of it all." She thought for a moment. "That all happened in North Platte: the divorce, her family, my dad's family … maybe Gabriel and I could find somebody there to talk to?"

"There you go!" Peter smiled as they finally reached his drive. He had no more than a wedge second on the 450 yard hole. After a moment's thought, he selected a club, waggled himself into his stance, and delivered a high pull that came to rest just a few feet from the runway left of the green. "Awe shucks," he muttered.

Hope watched as he picked up his small carry bag, slung it over his back, and started pushing his son down the fairway, smiling at Veeka. "That wasn't very good," she told him, "what happened?"

"I got greedy," Peter shrugged. "Tried too hard, jerked it way left."

"You'll probably make it from there!" Hope chuckled as she prepared to play her approach. It was a good lesson, she told herself. You had to stay within yourself. One of the hardest parts of golf was treating every shot as exactly what it was: nothing less and nothing more. She looked down at the small green and played a beautiful wedge to six feet.

"Maybe we can get you a public access show," Peter teased her, "the golfing preacher!"

"Great shot!" Veeka applauded. "Don't mind him, he's just jealous!" She stuck her tongue out at her husband.

Hope smiled at them. She loved their energy. "Maybe," she teased him back. "Maybe a televangelism show, like 'God wants you to buy me an airplane and a pilot so we can fly to Pebble Beach and play golf!'"

"See!" Peter laughed. "I told you she was one of *those* preachers! We're signing Irwin up for flight school right away!"

"Right," Veeka laughed back at him. "That's why she plays golf with us all the time. She's going to ask us for a million dollars! She's just waiting for the right moment."

Hope laughed back. She'd never meant to become a preacher. She'd never had much idea what sort of preacher she wanted to be. She still wasn't sure what kind of preacher she was. But if it turned out she was the kind of preacher whose primary religious experience was playing golf, she was pretty sure she was OK with that.

Five: Dougie
Third Green
Augusta National Golf Club
Augusta, Georgia

One of Dougie's strengths was not letting people get to him. It was one of the most important skills in the golf business. Once they saw you sweat, learned how to flip your switch, they'd never stop pushing you around. It was the first thing he looked for in hiring assistants. It was very rare, the ability to stand firm and take charge of a bunch of enraged alpha males by maintaining an air of lofty indifference and unspoken superiority. He'd realized long ago it wasn't the kind of thing he could ever teach anyone.

But this Chucky Kellerman! Dougie was starting to understand why he'd never seen Chucky visit Judge Smails in North Platte. It was hard to imagine them in the same room, hard to see how there'd be any oxygen for anyone else. Dad always said "If you think you know everything, you can never learn anything." Thirty minutes into their round, Dougie had no doubt Chucky knew everything, and no question how much he enjoyed sharing his wisdom.

"Twenty bucks says he don't finish five holes in double or less," Pork Chop McDonald stage-whispered to Dougie. They were standing just uphill of the third green, an L shaped puzzle that dropped sharply away from them to both front and back. They'd laid up well, to about 100 yards, and hit wedges to the back of the green, where they faced manageable uphill birdie putts.

Dougie looked over at the fourth tee, where the group in front of them was waiting. "You think maybe it wasn't pace of play he was worried about, back on the first tee?" Pork Chop snorted. He'd already had some sort of brush-up with Kellerman, in the middle of the second fairway. Dougie hadn't heard the details yet, but they'd squared off face to face, jabbing their fingers at each other.

"Yow!" There was a sudden yell. They looked down the hill across the green at the bunker below. A cloud of sand cleared. Chucky was standing in the middle of the bunker holding his right elbow. "It hit me!"

"You Maggerted yourself!" Chompers Turin chirped in from the other side of the sand trap. He looked up at Dougie and Pork Chop. "Jeff Maggert was leading here once, in the final round. He hit himself with a bunker shot, made triple, and never recovered! You're reliving history, Charlie!"

Chucky shook his arm a few times and looked around. "Yes, well, I guess we'll just call that a double then. You fellows go ahead and finish up." He picked up his ball, walked out of the bunker, and headed down towards the fourth tee. It was his third double in three holes. He'd actually had a bogey putt on the par 5 second, but he overpowered it past the hole and back off the green.

None of that bothered Dougie. Not one bit. Lots of people were bad at golf. Most of them were a lot of fun to play with. They didn't take themselves, or the game, too

seriously. You might even learn something from them.
The others, the ones who were hyperintense *and* horrible,
those were the ones Dougie had learned to avoid.

And Chucky, their host among the hallowed pines,
had to be one of the worst and most serious golfers Dougie
had ever played with. He watched Chompers play a
cautious little mid-iron bump-and-run up and over the
ridge, safely past the pin. Bill nodded to his caddie, took
his putter, and strode cheerfully up the hill. The dentist had
bogeyed the first two holes. Dougie was sure he'd be
perfectly happy to bogey every hole and shoot a smooth 90.
Odds were, he'd make a few pars along the way, maybe a
double, and wind up somewhere in the mid-80's. One of
Chompers' strengths was knowing who he was. He played
his own game, without apology.

Pork Chop would probably wind up a few shots back
of him, Dougie thought, even though he'd parred the
second and had a relatively friendly birdie putt here. For
whatever reason, Phil usually seemed to come up a few
shots short of Dr. Turin. Dougie even asked him about it
once. Pork Chop admitted sometimes he wanted to beat the
dentist so bad he got in his own way. "But," he added,
"Chompers and his grandkids are probably my best
customers, so I get most of it back anyway."

Bill and his wife Beth were the proud parents of nine
children. Five or six of their kids still lived in North Platte.
They had more grandkids than Dougie could count. Pizza

Gulch, Phil's casual place on Fourth Street, was their favorite family destination. Big Game, Phil's steakhouse on Second, was their fine dining favorite and the happy hour bar of choice for the Judge, Chief Riggs, Stewie Cottleston, and the rest of North Platte's movers and shakers.

Dr. Turin was a relative newcomer to North Platte and Bushwood. He'd moved his practice from Provo, Utah, just a little more than fifteen years ago. He and Beth joined Bushwood right away. At one of his first club events— Dougie thought it was the member-member—Bill went through the sandwich line three times. He'd been 'Dr. Chompers,' then just 'Chompers,' at Bushwood ever since.

The McDonalds, on the other hand, were as well-established a family as there was in North Platte. They'd had various restaurants in town for more than a hundred years. Big Game was a local institution, generally regarded as the best steak in town, which was a big deal in Nebraska. Phil was three or four years older than Dougie. People had called him 'Pork Chop' for as long as Dougie could remember, even back in high school where he was the biggest and strongest kid in town, a three-sport star athlete. Dougie actually took Phil's little sister Tammy to the junior prom once. He wasn't sure whether or not Phil remembered that. They'd never been really close friends.

Pork Chop was one of those members who liked to find little ways to remind Dougie that he was at Bushwood because he worked there, not because he was successful enough to join. It was strange—it wasn't like Dougie was so good at his job because he periodically forgot that he was at work—but it was just something some members did. It's what the Judge did when he called Dougie "my golf pro."

Dougie wasn't a regular with the Judge's group. They weren't that good, and the Judge wasn't the only one who fudged the rules. Over the last decade, he'd probably averaged two or three rounds a year with Chompers and maybe one or two with Pork Chop. He'd taken Chompers to a few pro-am events over the years. The dentist's conservative approach traveled well and he was easy to get along with. He couldn't remember Phil ever playing in any of those. Neither of them was at Bushwood every day. Not like the Judge. And now, after the Judge's passing, things with them were a little awkward.

The Judge, Dougie thought, wouldn't have been surprised. Not one bit. He'd make some smug remark, flash his leer of a smile, but he'd have a point. Maybe he didn't do it in the healthiest way, but the Judge really had been the glue that held Bushwood together. Now, without the Judge, here at Augusta, nobody knew quite what to do, what to say, how to act. Chompers and Pork Chop were tense and fidgety, mumbling at each other, not their usual confident selves. They seemed to be taking the Judge's death much harder than they had back home.

Dougie watched Pork Chop stand over his birdie putt just a little longer than normal, fidgeting back and forth. Not surprisingly, his putter 'exploded in his hands,' as Dad used to say, and his ball tracked up the hill well past the hole. Luckily, it stayed on their side of the mogul. If it had taken the corner to the right and started going down the other side, Dougie thought, it might well have rolled all the way down into a bunker. As it was, Pork Chop faced a nasty downhill par putt. Dougie saw him clench his putter even tighter and parse his lips, anger written across his whole face.

It made Dougie sad. He'd known Pork Chop, however casually, just about his whole life. He was usually relaxed, with a friendly smile for all. One of his strengths was his happy-go-lucky demeanor and devil-may-care attitude. On this trip, after the Judge's murder, he'd completely lost that. "Wow, that is fast even uphill" is all Dougie said. He looked over. The group on four was just starting to hit. He walked back up the hill to Pork Chop's ball. "Looks like they're not quick in front of us. Let's all relax." He let out a deep breath. "Let's take our time, maybe still take some good memories away from here."

"You bet!" Chompers agreed, nodding up and down. "We're here! Look at this place! Let's make the best of it!" He waved his arm over the pines towards Rae's Creek and shot Pork Chop a look, but the big man was gazing vacantly at the ground. Dougie looked at him for a second.

Pork Chop kept shaking his head and staring at the ground. It was the worst body language imaginable for putting on these greens.

Bending his neck, freeing himself from the moment, Dougie saw the path and walked back down to his ball. Stepping up into his line, he focused, relaxed, visualized and executed his putting stroke, reminding himself to power down through uphill putts. He looked up just in time to see his ball drop neatly in the hole. His first birdie at Augusta! He smiled and walked back up to the hole.

"That's beautiful Dougie!" Chompers acknowledged with a wave, already focusing on his par putt. "Great birdie!" Pork Chop's head was still buried in his chest, his putter tapping ominously against his shoes. Their group didn't have a game, but Dougie was pretty sure Phil and the dentist did. "Nobody plays for free," that's what they said in the Judge's group, even though they never played for more than a pittance.

He'd been a little surprised when Chucky hadn't said anything about a game on the first tee. After watching their host butcher the first three holes, though, Dougie understood. For his part, Dougie, who'd managed two routine pars and now this birdie, playing Augusta, under par, felt about as good as anything else he could imagine right now. Even the Judge couldn't quarrel with that!

Chompers side-stepped himself into his tense, knock-kneed stance, carefully made two practice strokes, his tongue slithering in and out of his mouth, and hit his putt, extending his upper body far down the line of the putt, almost dancing towards the hole, in his trademark exaggerated follow-through. It worked this time. The dentist's ball bounced off the back of the cup and dropped in for par.

"Nice putt Bill!" Dougie congratulated him. "Phil, did you see that?"

Pork Chop looked up. "I saw it." A strained smile crawled across his face. "Nice putt Chompers. That's a heck of a par from down there!"

"Thanks," the dentist acknowledged. "I'm rooting for you on this one—got to keep things interesting!"

"Screw you. Don't do me any favors," Pork Chop growled as he examined his putt, "except maybe you take Kellerman out into the pines and only one of you comes back."

"He is annoying," Dougie agreed. "I can't imagine how he was friends with the Judge. But don't let him ruin this! You guys said we'd still do this. You said you wanted to come all this way. You said it's what the Judge would have wanted. Well, I guess the Judge would have wanted us to put up with this guy, to see in him what the Judge saw in him."

"The Judge hated Kellerman," Pork Chop scowled. "He knew what a prick he was." He stood up from his putt. "C'mon Dougie, you know what the Judge saw in him: he saw opportunity. The same thing that bastard saw in everyone. All Smails ever cared about was greasing his own sausage. If Kellerman, or you, or me, or anyone else, could help him, if we had something he wanted, if we could do something for him, he'd turn on the charm and ratchet up the pressure. Doesn't mean Smails liked him, or me, or you, or anyone but himself."

"You think the Judge would ever have admitted his old law school buddy who could get him on here was a whiny annoying stuffed shirt who couldn't break 100?" Chompers added. "I know I didn't know him as long as you two, but I knew Smails more than enough to know he was in it 100% for Smails, whatever it was."

"OK," Dougie admitted, "it's no big secret the Judge dipped his hands in a lot of pockets. But what's that got to do with Kellerman? He's some big shot New York lawyer, went to school with the Judge. What could the Judge do for him? Other than getting him on here, what could Kellerman do for the Judge?"

Chompers looked at Pork Chop but the big man was staring down at the ground again. "Who do you think … No, better question, Dougie: Why do you think Smails got murdered?" The dentist looked calmly at Dougie like discussing who killed Judge Smails was a perfectly normal conversation to have on the third green at Augusta.

"Why did he get killed? What do you mean?" Dougie started, nervously twitching back and forth.

"Because somebody killed him! I guess. I mean, I don't know. Criminals! You probably know what people are saying, maybe better than I do. Could be somebody the Judge sentenced, they got out of jail and wanted revenge, something like that. Might be somebody was trying to rob him." He stopped and looked at them. "I'm sure you've heard people talking about Ivanka, just like everyone has."

The Judge was married to his first wife Pookie, the daughter of a powerful local ranching family, for more than forty years. She died in a freak accident at the state fair three or four years ago. One of the cars flew off of the Orbiter ride and careened down the midway, crushing six people.

A few months later, the Judge showed up at Bushwood out of the blue one day with a new wife. Ivanka Smails was born in the Ukraine. She was a lot younger than the Judge and, at least to hear the Judge tell it, could hardly keep her hands off of him long enough for him to play golf. Pookie's Bushwood friends hadn't taken kindly to her, to say the least. The Judge either didn't care or pretended not to notice. Maybe both. Ivanka didn't play golf. Dougie didn't really know her at all, didn't know if she had any real friends in North Platte.

Pork Chop shook his head. "Never did understand her, don't even really know her, but … and, I'm not saying she didn't do it, but she's what, maybe 100 pounds? How could a woman her size shove something as big as that shower rod down the Judge's throat? He may have been old, but he wasn't feeble. Not without help, she couldn't." The big man shook his head again.

"Riggs didn't say anything to me about her," Dougie added. "But other people have. Mostly just, like you say, nobody really knows her. Nobody really knows anything about her. I think a lot of people still resent her because, well, because of Pookie I guess."

"And I'm not saying I'd have let any of my daughters marry the Judge either," Chompers added. "Who knows how miserable that might have been for her?"

The people who'd speculated about Ivanka to Dougie had focused more on the Judge's money than her misery, but at the same time Pork Chop had a point. She was a tiny woman and the Judge was a strong man.

"So sure, being married to the Judge could have been miserable," Chompers continued. "Sure, the Judge liked to hand out harsh sentences. Those could all be reasons for somebody to kill the Judge. I'm not saying they're not. But, on the other hand, you have to ask: were there any other people might have had other reasons for wanting him dead, anyone who might have profited from his death?"

"What are you saying? Are you saying Kellerman killed Smails?" Dougie looked at Pork Chop. "Is that what you two were squabbling about, back there on two?"

"Guys like Kellerman," Pork Chop spat on the green, "they don't kill people themselves. Like they don't mop their own kitchens. They hire people.”

“A hit man!” Dougie raised his voice and Chompers reached over to settle him down.

“Nobody’s saying that,” the dentist assured him. “Phil’s just … We’re all just a bit upset right now. Let’s stay calm. Let’s not make any hasty accusations.” He nodded at Pork Chop to putt.

“No,” Dougie nodded, “no, that’s what Chief Riggs said! He said it was somebody who knew him, who knew the Judge. That or it was a professional hit man! I didn’t think anything of it. I just assumed his murder didn’t have anything to do with … well, with me. With golf, I guess.”

“Nobody’s saying it does,” Chompers re-assured him. “But Dougie, you have to admit, there wasn’t much of Smails’ life, not even Ivanka, that didn’t have *anything* to do with golf.”

“He gave lighter sentences to golfers,” Pork Chop added. “Didn’t matter who they were, what they’d done. They played golf, the Judge was their friend. He’d hand them 20 years with ‘six months credit for time served,’ even if they ‘d only been in jail a week, just cause they were golfers.” The big man wiggled his putter back and forth over his ball. “Course, most judges would only have given them 10 years in the first place. He was a vengeful bastard, but he did love his golf.”

“So why was he killed?” It was hard for Dougie to accept that golf could have played any part in the Judge’s murder. But they had a point. Golf had been so central to the Judge's life that it would be strange for it to be totally absent from his death.

Dougie was sure Chompers had a theory, but the dentist stayed silent as Phil stepped over his ball. This time he stayed in his rhythm. He barely started his ball moving down the slope. It tracked perfectly and tumbled into the center of the cup.

"Just another routine par!" Chompers congratulated him.

"Wow!" Dougie added. "That's the shot of the day so far. Great putt!"

Pork Chop stood up. He gave them a faint smile and started down to pick up his ball. "Why did he get killed? Somebody decided they'd be better off with him dead. Someone decided killing Smails was worth the risk of getting caught."

Six: Bison
Tenth Tee
Golf Club of Houston – Tournament Course
Humble, Texas

"You're going to win the Masters!" Even for Big Poppa, that was a whopper. He hadn't said anything like that again. But he'd been on quite a roll none the less. Bison had never seen Big Poppa so happy. He'd relocated them from the Woodlands to even more luxurious rooms— penthouse suites—at a historic 1920s era boutique hotel in the Theater District with its own Texas art collection. They hadn't seen any shows, but the marble shower and nighttime views of the city were pretty amazing. Bison enjoyed wandering around after dinner marveling at the paintings of longhorns and live oaks.

Big Poppa even put Hamilton, who'd acquired a second job as their driver, up at the hotel with them, albeit in a single room. The kid still didn't say very much, but he'd proved nothing but reliable. He certainly drove better than Big Poppa.

They hadn't ever had much of a talk about caddying after the Monday qualifier at Cypresswood. Big Poppa had been so enthusiastic and joyful that Bison couldn't bring himself to say anything about maybe looking for somebody with more experience. And now here they were, getting ready to tee off in their first full tournament together: his first PGA Tour round in almost four years. He still hadn't paid Hamilton anything himself, and they'd never really talked about the terms of his employment. Big Poppa, who'd hired Hamilton in the first place, was taking care of him just fine. Bison wasn't worried about Hamilton, at least until Big Poppa's money ran out, as it inevitably would.

But it meant Hamilton was, for now at least, working for Big Poppa, not for him. At the moment, with everything peaches and gravy, that didn't mean a thing. Bison couldn't see exactly how it might cause trouble down the road. But it was out there. It was out of his control. And it would change if he made the cut, putting Hamilton in position for an as-yet unspecified bonus share.

Feeling complete control and worry free is what makes champions. Bison knew the world was full of guys with great swings who could hit impossible shots and hole clutch putts. Thousands were gifted with the tools. But the greats, the multi-millionaires with decades-long careers, they didn't leave themselves any room for questions to creep in. They didn't brush over details like how much their caddie made. They knew that it's impossible to play championship golf while you're questioning yourself.

There are a lot of ways to stop questioning yourself, just like there are different ways to swing the golf club. Guys like Bernhard Langer and Bubba Watson tapped into a higher power, finding control through faith. Others, like Tom Kite and Vijay Singh, found control in hard work and endless repetition, beating their questions out of the dirt like Hogan did. Bison wanted to see himself in that mold, but he wasn't sure he practiced enough, which is to say he still asked himself too many questions.

But here he was, standing on the tenth tee with Zach Sukert, a handsome young journeyman who'd been part of a Backstreet Boys cover band before turning pro, and John Merritt. Bison had played with Merritt more than a few times before. The tour paired people by matching up their career trajectories: both of them had managed a single tour victory several years ago and struggled thereafter. Merritt could be challenging. They shook hands with a minimum of courtesies.

Bison didn't care. Nothing was going to bother him today. Not Merritt, not Hamilton, not if Sukert started singing and dancing. Not three-putting every hole and shooting 90. Not a thing. It was a beautiful day, the golf course was in great shape, and he was still jacked up from qualifying. It felt great to be back on tour. He was playing well. He really believed in his action. He waggled his driver back and forth a few times, watching Hamilton count clubs and reinventory the pockets of their bag.

Bison looked down the fairway, waiting for the starter to release their group. The tenth was an uncomplicated par 4 with a generous fairway. He expected to have a birdie opportunity. He looked over the small gallery. People were mostly just arriving, mulling around the clubhouse, figuring out where to go. Very few, if any, were paying much attention to their group. He saw Big Poppa standing on the patio, waving his cane in the air. His smile was larger than ever. Bison smiled back and gave him a confident little wave. What a great day!

"Will you please welcome to the tenth tee," he heard the starter say, "the 7:37 starting time. From Birmingham Alabama, Zach Sukert." The handsome young southerner doffed his cap neatly towards the sparse crowd and drove his ball nicely down the left side. "From Long Beach California, John Merritt."

Merritt wasn't a complete jerk. At least, that's what people always said. Someone told Bison once that if Merritt had been from Dallas or Philadelphia, nobody would ever have had a problem with him. Merritt certainly didn't act like he was from Southern California. It was just one more little thing about him that jostled people's sensibilities. He was never quite what people expected him to be.

Whatever else he was, Merritt was an exceptional driver of the ball. This tee shot posed no real challenge for him. But, as Bison knew he would, the tanned veteran went methodically through his detailed pre-shot routine. He wasn't really slow, Bison reflected, just really, really deliberate. He broke every movement down into its smallest components. As his jittery staccato maneuvering continued, everything seemed to blur together and start taking longer than it really did. But at the end of it all,

Merritt's ball tracked straight down the middle of the fairway. Bison expected he'd repeat the exact same process, with pretty much the same result, all morning.

"From Trophy Club Texas, Bison Tromble." The tour let you say you were "from" anywhere you wanted. Some guys were "from" places they hadn't lived in decades. Technically, Bison's apartment was in Southlake, a less opulent suburb a little closer to DFW airport. But Trophy Club, the only course Hogan ever designed, was the closest golf club, and they'd been kind enough to let him hit balls there a few times, so he didn't consider it a total lie. He thought it sounded more successful.

Bison touched his cap and looked out at the crowd again. Big Poppa was doing a little dance up and down the patio steps, raising his arms and bowing his head up and down. Holding his cane in the air, he looked like a scarecrow, or some sort of strange shaman. Bison smiled and looked over at the first tee, where a larger gallery had gathered. He glanced down the fairway. It might as well have been a million miles wide.

Bison stepped into his stance. He looked out at his target, the right edge of a pine tree. In the corner of his eye, he saw Merritt digging into a pocket of his bag. He backed up and started over. Merritt was so jittery and self-absorbed that sometimes he didn't stay as still as he should. Fidgety and deliberate could be a challenging combination to play with. Bison had never heard of anyone accusing

Merritt of cheating, or even gamesmanship, of ever deliberately trying to influence play. He was just wound a bit tighter and wrapped up in himself a lot more than most. Merritt did a lot of little things differently. If a couple of them bothered someone, it could make for a long round.

Bison shrugged it off and stepped back in. He felt great. He whipped the club smoothly around his yoke and drove it through the ball. It felt tremendous. The sound was beautiful. He looked up and saw his ball heading down the middle of the fairway, exactly on line with the tree branch he'd aimed at. Amid the polite claps, he heard Big Poppa call out "One in a row!" He smiled. "One at a time," he told Hamilton, handing him the driver.

Hamilton smiled. He replaced the headcover and hoisted their bag. "One down," he told Bison casually, "two hundred and sixty-two to go." He held Bison's eyes firmly in his gaze for an extra moment, as if marking the moment in their memories, before turning and hurrying down the fairway behind Merritt's caddie Dodger, an old-school Scot who'd been out on tour for decades.

Bison hesitated a moment. Questions started swirling up inside him. "Here we go!" He looked up and saw Big Poppa standing just outside the ropes. "Here we go now, here we go!" It was something he used to sing to them when Hope was a baby, to get them up and moving. "Here we go now, here we go!" Big Poppa marched out down the fairway chanting and clapping his cane against the ground, drawing Bison along in his wake.

Bison shook his head and started walking towards his drive. He saw Hamilton catch up to Dodger, a few steps behind Merritt, and right away start nodding his head vigorously at the veteran caddie. Bison couldn't remember everyone Dodger had worked for, but he was pretty sure he'd been in the thick of things at a few majors. Any tips Hamilton could squeeze out of Dodger would be great.

The gallery did not follow them as they moved away from the clubhouse. Big Poppa slowed down to a normal pace and stopped waving. Bison felt his first tee adrenalin rush subside as he settled into the rhythm of his steps. It felt great to be on the course. By the time they reached their drives, there were only three or four spectators with them. Sukert and Merritt were about 100 yards from the hole, with Bison fifteen yards or so past them.

"I think it's you," Bison heard Merritt tell Sukert, who shot him a surprised look. Usually a glance, maybe a hand waved across the fairway, was all that was needed to determine the order of play. And if guys did say something, it was almost always in the form of a question, like "who is it?" It was another case of Merritt not being exactly rude, but different. Bison wondered if Sukert had played with Merritt before. He hoped the young southerner would be patient and play well.

Playing well makes everything easier. It's hard to be really upset after making birdie. The better Sukert played, the less likely Merritt's idiosyncrasies would bother him. And, everything else being equal, it's easier to play well alongside others who are playing well. Watching good shots is a lot healthier for the mind than watching bad ones. Rooting for your fellow competitors, especially in the first round, was more than just good sportsmanship. It was good strategy. At least that's how Bison looked at it. Others were more cutthroat or just indifferent, like Merritt.

Watching Sukert fidget over his wedge shot and glance back and forth at Merritt, Bison wasn't sure how that theory would play out in this group today. Finally, Sukert came all the way up out of his stance and went back to his bag. "Good move Zach," Bison heard Sukert's caddie Ryan say. "Trust your routine. Find your focus. It's just you and the hole."

Merritt fidgeted with his club while Sukert replayed his process and set up over his ball. His swing was just a touch faster than it had been on the tee though, and he pulled his wedge left into a bunker. It was a poor result on such a forgiving hole and Sukert knew it.

"It's you now then," Bison heard Sukert tell Merritt, his irritation clear over his southern twang, but the Californian had already tuned out everything but his jerky pre-shot dance and focused on a small circle around the hole. He hit a good shot to about fifteen feet and reached back without looking to take his putter from Dodger.

"Nice shot John," Bison said politely. No reply was

forthcoming. Hamilton set their bag down next to his drive. He saw Sukert standing by the gallery ropes on the left, near Big Poppa, talking quietly to his caddie, his head nodding up and down.

"79 front, 87 pin," Hamilton said as Bison reached in the bag for his wedge.

"You sure?" Bison asked. It was the first yardage the teenager had ever given him. All of a sudden, he sounded like he'd been out here for years. Bison looked over at Big Poppa on the side of the fairway, nodding and tapping his cane up and down between his feet. He looked back at Hamilton, who held up his yardage book and smiled.

"Absolutely!" Hamilton nodded. "I've got this course wired. Nothing to it! It's just math. I walked this off from two different spots." He smiled at Bison. "I learn fast. You just relax and hit good shots."

"OK," Bison smiled. He looked up at the flag and felt the early morning sun on his face. It felt great. He stepped into his stance and whipped the wedge around his yoke. "Oh, get close," he muttered as he watched the ball fly towards the green. It felt as good as his drive. It looked like it was going to hit the pin.

"One in a row!" he heard Big Poppa shout from the edge of the fairway as his ball landed five feet long and spun back off the lip of the hole to about six inches. It looked like he'd missed the flag in the air by just an inch or two, and then come even closer to holing out as the ball backed up.

"Nice shot!" Sukert congratulated him from the side of the fairway. Bison looked over and saw Sukert smiling. He heard polite clapping from the fifteen or twenty people watching around the green. Merritt stayed silent and strode out ahead of them towards the green, his expression unchanged.

"Thanks Zach," Bison acknowledged as he took his putter from Hamilton and followed Merritt towards the green. 87 was the perfect yardage. He wondered for a moment what Hamilton might do next, but realized there was nothing he could do about it. "Keep up the good work," he said without looking back.

When they got to the green, Sukert found his ball half-buried in the face of the bunker. He shook his head a few times. He kicked the bottom of his bag before pulling a club and walking down into the sand, obviously flustered.

"You got this!" Bison heard Big Poppa encourage the young pro. He looked over while he was marking his ball and saw that Big Poppa had taken up a position near the path to the eleventh tee. Once again he was almost dancing, nodding his head back and forth and tapping his cane up and down on the ground. "Easy shot!"

Bison saw Sukert look up from the bunker at the sound of Big Poppa's voice. The Southerner smiled when he saw Big Poppa bopping up and down on the other side of the green. He visibly relaxed. His hands snapped his wedge back and forth with more authority. Bison could practically see his confidence grow as he settled into his stance. Taking almost a full swing, he stabbed the club violently into the sand behind the ball. It popped out softly, landed neatly on the edge of the green, and rolled out just a couple of feet past the hole.

"That a boy! Great shot!" Big Poppa clapped loudly. Sukert raised his club to acknowledge his support.

"Great shot Zach!" Bison added. "That's as good as it gets from there. Wonderful stuff!"

"Thanks, thanks everyone," Sukert said as he climbed out of the bunker and tapped the sand off of his shoes. He took his putter and walked over to mark his ball while Merritt started reading the green. Bison was surprised to see Hamilton step forward with his towel in his hands, making himself available to clean Sukert's ball while Ryan raked the bunker. It was one of the little ways caddies helped each other. He had no idea where or how Hamilton had learned it. He looked over at Big Poppa, but he was still celebrating Sukert's brilliant bunker shot.

Sukert waved Hamilton off and pocketed his ball as Merritt stalked his birdie putt. He fidgeted back and forth from his ball to the hole a few times, called Dodger over for a brief consultation, and slowly took up his position. Bison saw Big Poppa shaking his head disapprovingly at Merritt, whose back was to him, and slowly rocking back and forth, like there was music only he could hear.

Merritt, who was not a great putter, stroked quickly back and through and missed badly, leaving it a full three feet short and just behind Sukert's marker. Bison looked over at Sukert, whose left hand came up to cover his mouth, and knew instantly what had flashed through Zach's mind: 'You're still away!'

But nobody said anything. Sukert walked over and moved his mark. Merritt fidgeted back and forth around the hole before settling in for his second putt. Big Poppa seemingly didn't miss a beat, leaning back and forth behind Merritt's back. Merritt overcompensated and jerked it long left for a demoralizing three-putt bogey.

Zach replaced his marker and confidently rapped his putt into the back of the hole. He bent over, picked it up, and quickly lifted it in the air, nodding again towards Big Poppa. Bison replaced his ball. He had a special routine for putts under a foot, reminding himself to take the simple task seriously, and he tapped in without incident.

"One in a row!" Big Poppa called out. "Can't birdie 'em all unless you birdie the first!"

"Nice birdie," Sukert said. Merritt lifted his hand in perfunctory acknowledgment as he walked past Big Poppa and up the path to eleven with Sukert following.

Bison lifted his ball out of the hole and held it up as a brief wave of applause ran through the tiny gallery. He remembered now. That was what winning felt like!

"On to the next!" Hamilton smiled as he took the

putter and handed Bison his driver. "You got this!"

"Yep," Bison nodded, smiling in spite of himself. "I got this!" He gave Big Poppa a quick fist-bump as they followed Sukert's caddie Ryan, who'd just finished raking the bunker, up the path towards the eleventh tee.

"You and your caddie just keep your mouths off my ball!" Bison heard. He turned the corner to see Merritt gesturing angrily at Sukert. "I heard what he said in the bunker there!"

"What did he say?" Sukert shot right back.

"You know darn well what he said."

"No, No! I'm not sure he said anything. You just look out for yourself!" Sukert, who'd been so emboldened by his spectacular bunker shot, was visibly trembling with anger. Merritt, who was tense and fidgety at the best of times, was red in the face. Beads of sweat were dripping down his forehead.

For a moment, Bison thought they were going to come to blows. He saw that the fairway was clear, but hesitated, not wanting to provoke them. But after a long tense moment, both players backed down ever so slightly. Seizing the moment, Bison walked forward and took the tee. It was surprisingly easy for him to put their squabble out of mind and focus on the spot where his drive would cut though the dogleg. That's what champions did.

Seven: Danny
Seventh Tee
Augusta National Golf Club
Augusta, Georgia

This was turning into the strangest round of golf Danny had ever played. Here he was, three under through six at Augusta. Maybe it was from these members tees, which took away a lot of the challenge and most of the glory, but still: three under was three under. He'd stuffed a wedge and tapped in on one. He'd reached the second in two and two-putted. Just a moment ago, he'd somehow holed one of the best putts of his life, a thirty-footer from the middle of the sixth green back down to the front left pin. It seemed like it took five minutes to crawl down that hill into the hole! He'd made smart, professional two-putt pars from the middle of the greens on four and five, two of the hardest holes in major championship golf. Those holes were still plenty tough from these tees. Danny had it going!

None of it mattered. It hadn't made the slightest dent on his world. Nobody had even noticed, let alone cared, except maybe Tobias. Tobias was really enjoying himself. "Man that was a fine putt," he was telling the other caddies. "How many times you seen somebody make that?" But Danny had a feeling Tobias might enjoy himself just as much if he hit five balls in the water. "How many times you see that? Just like that movie! My man Don Johnson!" Tobias struck him as somebody who'd found his way to a profession where he enjoyed himself no matter what happened at his work.

Danny liked working hard but never saw much point in working for other people. He hadn't had a regular job since he parked cars at Circus Circus for a few weeks right after he turned twenty-one, the first time he moved to Vegas. He hadn't enjoyed that at all. He didn't feel like he was missing out on much of anything now by not working.

Danny made his money by reading people. That was one of his strongest gifts. Given a few hours to watch somebody go about their business, he'd usually get a pretty good feel for what made them tick. After that, he could predict how they'd respond to different things. Then it was just a matter of watching and waiting for them to be in the right situation, where he'd know what they were going to do before they did.

Over the years he'd learned that people like Tobias, who always enjoyed themselves at work, were generally pretty good, but not great, at their jobs. They were typically calm and steady, competent and easy to be around. Sometimes, though, they'd settled so far into their jobs, gotten so comfortable, that they could be thinking anything behind their same pleasant smiles. That's the read Danny had on Tobias: that he'd be pleasant and competent and enjoy their round no matter what happened, but there was little or no chance of him ever sharing his true feelings.

These two fat angry lawyers he'd been condemned to

play with, on the other hand, were just exactly the opposite of Tobias in every respect. They were determined to be miserable no matter what happened. They didn't hold anything back. They weren't the least bit shy about sharing their woes or airing their grievances. And they weren't even at work!

Or maybe they were. It was hard to tell, Danny thought. They'd certainly thrown a fair bit of legal jargon back and forth. They definitely weren't here to play golf. Once they got ten or fifteen feet from the hole, they slapped casually at the ball and waved their caddie in to pick it up, no matter the result. He wasn't sure either of them had actually recorded a score on any of the first six holes. Neither of them had displayed much interest in or passion for the game.

But they sure knew a lot about Judge Smails! Danny hadn't been back to North Platte for more than a long weekend in decades. He'd barely kept up with Dad, much less Dougie, for most of his life. He could honestly say he'd never wondered a single time whatever happened to that crazy Judge Smails. Now, playing for the first time this course he'd been so obsessed with as a boy, he'd spent the last ninety minutes involuntarily enrolled in a symposium on the Judge's life and murder.

The idea of playing golf at Augusta National just to have a convenient excuse for talking about Judge Smails' murder was hard for Danny to wrap his mind around. But it was impossible for him to completely tune out the two cackling lawyers. So he couldn't help learning a lot, even if he was only mildly interested, at least at the beginning, because it soon became obvious the only reason either of them was here was to talk about Smails.

Danny learned that the Judge's first wife was killed in a freak amusement park accident just a few years ago. He learned that the Judge, in his grief, remarried shortly after her death. He learned that the townsfolk, especially the ladies of Bushwood, vehemently disapproved of the Judge's second wife, who was a younger, more sexually charged woman from Eastern Europe.

"God those shrews hated him for her," Stewie told Smiley back on the first green. "They hated seeing him so happy. They hated how much he told their husbands, sharing vulgar details like he did all the time, bragging about her. They were scared of him!"

"Scared of their husbands, more like it," Smiley had replied. "God forbid any of them start thinking about doing what the Judge did. But that doesn't mean she didn't do it!" Smiley, Danny learned right away, was sure that the Judge's second wife, having grown more and more weary of being pawed, flaunted, and intimately described to the Bushwood locker room by her loving husband the Judge, had sought her own naked justice in their shower. "Who else could have been in the shower with him naked?" That, for Smiley, was the crux of the matter, the beginning and the end of the mystery. Only his lusty new bride could have been with the Judge naked in their shower, where he was killed, so only she could have killed him.

As they'd waited for the second green to clear so Danny could hit his second, Stewie vehemently disputed Smiley's theory. "She signed the pre-nup!" That's what he kept saying. "She's not that stupid!" Stewie, Danny learned, "wrote the damn pre-nup." The legal and financial consequences of the Judge's fall for his lusty young widow were drastic and immediate. "She'll be lucky if she can buy a one-way ticket back to Kiev after this," Stewie opined. "Whether she did it or not, the Judge's murder is not going to work out well for her. Why would she do that to herself?"

"Everyone has a breaking point," Smiley countered. "I'm not saying she thought she was going to get away with it. Maybe she didn't think about it at all, just grabbed that shower rod and kept his damn hands off of her for once and for all. Maybe she'll plead self-defense, say he was abusing her. Does she have a lawyer?"

"She doesn't need one yet. They haven't arrested her,"

"But there aren't any other suspects!" Smiley insisted. "They're gonna have to arrest her pretty soon, unless somebody else confesses, some other evidence turns up."

"Maybe," Stewie admitted. "I can't say for sure it

wasn't her. But I can't see how that makes any sense.
She's a big girl. She knew what she was getting with the
Judge. She got her Mercedes, her credit cards, maid
service. She always seemed happy enough with the Judge,
not sure why she'd do a 180 on him now."

After that, they'd spent a few holes discussing various
affairs the Judge had during his first marriage. Several
cuckolded husbands were mocked, with varying degrees of
sympathy and disrespect, and considered as possible
suspects. In the end, Stewie and Smiley agreed it was
unlikely any vengeful husband would wait for years to
claim his revenge. Stewie made emphatic and vulgar
assurances that the Judge hadn't cheated on his second wife
even once because "that would have been more than the
man was capable of."

Then they talked for a while about different criminal
and civil matters Smails had adjudicated, speculating
whether any recipients of the Judge's justice might have
done him in. Stewie told stories about the Judge's biggest
cases, which meant Smiley had to tell stories about his
biggest cases, so as not to let his deceased classmate
outshine him. In the end, neither of them seemed to think
any of the Judge's unsatisfied customers carried the kind of
hatred for Smails that would lead to death by shower rod.

Walking down the big hill to the sixth green, that led
Smiley right back to the second Mrs. Smails. "You can't
even think of any other suspects! It must have been her.

Just tell me one thing: who else could have been in that shower? How is there any point in even talking about anyone else unless they could have been in that shower?"

"What about her alibi?" Stewie countered. "She does have a pretty good alibi, being in another state and all."

"With her family in Colorado?" Smiley scoffed. "Please. Like they're going to say she wasn't there?" Mrs. Smails the younger, Danny learned while he was lining up his twisting downhill birdie triumph, had two cousins living in Edgewater, just outside of Denver. She'd visited them there the last week of March, during spring break, every year since she'd married the Judge. She'd come home from Edgewater the day after they'd found the Judge's body.

Smiley paid her story little mind. "It's only a three or four hour drive, right?" Stewie admitted it was. "So she would have had plenty of time to put the kids to bed, drive to North Platte, lure the Judge into the shower, do the deed, and drive back in time to wake up and have breakfast in Colorado with her family?" Years ago, Danny had driven back and forth from Vegas to Chicago on that exact route through Edgewater and North Platte several times. As he settled in over his birdie putt, he had to admit Smiley had a point. It was all wide open high plains freeway, an easy drive.

"But she went there every year," Stewie insisted. "Are you saying she started planning this on her wedding day?" Danny watched his putt dribble down the ridge as the lawyers kept jabbering.

"Who knows," Smiley answered as Danny's ball tippled in. "You're the one says you don't really know anything about her, even though you 'wrote the damn pre-nup.' You're the one who saw the Judge every day, but somehow never saw this coming. Maybe she planned it from the start, maybe she just realized how convenient it was, how should I know? You were there! And you're still not convincing me the Judge let anyone else in that damn shower with him, not that you have the slightest idea who it might have been."

That shut Stewie up. At least for the moment it did. But Danny saw right away the redhead hadn't appreciated Smiley's criticisms. He'd seen the edges of Stewie's face start turning red as they walked up the hill to the seventh tee. Dougie's group was still in the fairway waiting to hit their second, or maybe third, shots, so they'd waited on the tee in stony quiet for a few minutes. After six holes of non-stop Judge Smails talk, the silence was refreshing at first. As they waited, however, it started growing more and more ominous. Danny hoped Sterno wasn't about to erupt.

As Dougie's group finally started moving forward, Tobias walked up to the tee with Danny's driver, four iron, and sand wedge.

"I can only hit one of those," Danny deadpanned.

"Who says!" Tobias laughed. "They say you

shouldn't tell yourself you can't do things."

"They say a lot of things." Danny looked at the three clubs. "You think sand wedge might be a good play here?"

"I think it don't matter *what* you hit here." Tobias looked over at Smiley and Stewie fidgeting angrily and carefully looking away from each other. "I don't know what's going on with them, don't remember this Judge of yours, don't know who killed him. Sounds to me like he had it coming. Don't care who killed him any more than they care about playing golf."

"Or any more than I care about them," Danny nodded. "So what? I'm still here, playing my own game."

"Sure," Tobias nodded. "You're doing a fine job of that! Question is: what game do you want to play here by yourself?" He had a big smile on his face.

"OK," Danny grinned back. "I'll bite. What game do I play with the sand wedge here?"

"That's the Fred Couples game," Tobias replied without hesitation. "He tells stories all the time about when he used to get bored playing with chops, he'd play the par 4 holes backwards: hit sand wedges off the tees and three wood approaches." Tobias pointed out to the fairway. "You hit sand wedge here, I bet it leaves you a perfect three wood distance!" His smile grew even bigger. "Only five traps around that green, wouldn't take much of a three wood shot at all!"

"No," Danny laughed. "No," he repeated in a mock-serious tone, "no, that would be much too easy. What else you got?"

Tobias held up his four iron. "If you absolutely had to make birdie," the veteran told him, "this is what we'd hit. We hit this great on three. You hit that same shot again here, it leaves us more or less the same distance we had on one. This pin is harder, but that's a great distance for you."

"OK," Danny nodded. "That sounds like the play. So why do you have the driver? Why be closer? Thirty yards short, over those bunkers … that might be tougher than the three wood second shot!"

"That's what you asked for," Tobias grinned. "Sure. It might well be. But from this tee, you can drive that green. Byron Nelson did it. In 1937. Said it was the best round of golf he ever played." He took Danny's driver and pointed down the Georgia pines lining the left side. "Remember where the third tee is, back past all those trees?"

Danny followed the line of the club. He looked up through the trees to their left. The third fairway ran back up the hill away from Rae's Creek and turned slightly to the right, so you couldn't see that green from here. But he could make out where the second green was through the trees, and the third tee was just steps behind that. "OK, I got it."

"The last tree on the left, you can't see it, but it's about 275. You hit a draw that bounces off the upslope just right of that tree, either on the fly or on the first bounce, don't matter either way. You hit that, it jumps up the hill towards the second green, catches a slot, and feeds back down between the bunkers onto the green. You catch that slot right, ball might roll 75 or 80 yards."

"And if you don't?" Danny looked at Tobias. "If I miss that slot, best thing that could happen would be for it to roll down into the bottom of one of those front bunkers. That's just a hard shot. What happens if I leave it under a tree or 45 yards short on the downhill?"

"That would be bad," Tobias acknowledged. "You'd have to hit a great shot from there. Or putt around the bunker and take your five. Like I said, if you had to make birdie, we'd hit the four iron. But, on the other hand, you draw it up that slot, you might have the memory of driving this green for the rest of your life. Up to you, whether or not that's worth the risk of not making another birdie nobody else gives a crap about." Tobias glanced over at Stewie and Smiley, who were still avoiding eye contact, and back down at their caddies, who had their backs turned. Tobias looked him in the eyes and held out his driver. "Take the shot!"

Danny looked down at the three clubs and back up towards the green. Dougie's group was still putting. He took the driver from Tobias and waggled it back and forth a few times, watching Dougie walk back and forth.

"Don't worry about them," Tobias told him. "No

chance that ball gets there with enough speed to hurt anyone."

Danny nodded, focusing in on the slope just right of the last tree on the left. He couldn't fly it there, but he felt like it was well within bouncing range. He thought about the four iron he'd hit on three. He had no urge to hit that shot again. Tobias was right. It didn't really matter what he did today. Take the shot.

Danny settled in over his ball, enjoying the silence that had settled over Smiley and Stewie. When he pictured it bouncing up Tobias's slot, he let the club follow that path back and through. He made good contact, but felt the ball draw just a fraction more than he'd intended. It landed about ten yards left of his line and well short of the last tree, bouncing under the trees and running up the hill towards the left side of the second green. He didn't see it come back down the hill.

"That'll be fine," Tobias assured him. "Missed the slot to get home, but there's a lot of level ground there, short of the bunker on two."

Danny nodded and handed him the driver. Stewie and Smiley stepped up and hit nearly matching slices down the right side, the redhead about 45 yards further into the pines.

Danny followed Tobias up the left side of the fairway, under the pines, and tried to imagine deciding to kill somebody who wasn't trying to kill him. It was hard. Life was such a gift. Karma was so real. Danny assumed he, like anyone, had some sort of breaking point past which he might lash out in a mindless rage and take a life. But standing here on these hallowed fairways under the Georgia sun he could not for the life of him conceive of any scenario where murdering anyone would ever sound like a good plan.

Tobias stopped a few yards ahead of Smiley's drive, which had taken a fortuitous bounce off a pine tree back towards the fairway. "Membership has its privileges," they heard Stewie remark disparagingly as he walked into the woods further right to search for his drive.

"So does not being a dumbass," Smiley retorted.

"Who's the dumbass," Stewie turned back uphill and put his hands on his hips, "who assured us all that the Judge was good for the money, that he didn't need to tell any of us any of the particulars! Who's the dumbass," he continued, his voice rising, "who said giving the Judge half a million dollars without knowing where any of it was going was a good idea?"

"Who's the dumbass," Smiley shouted back, "who was right there with him every day? Who's the dumbass who laughed obsequiously at his horseshit stories and drank his cheap scotch at that same crappy steakhouse every day?" They stared at each other. "Who's the dumbass who doesn't know where our money is?"

Eight: Hope
Fifteenth Fairway
River's Edge Golf Club
North Platte, Nebraska

Gabriel had never played eighteen holes before. He'd never played anywhere but Shelter Cove before. He'd never been further away from home than San Francisco before. He'd never known anything about her side of the family before. Given all that, Hope felt like he was actually doing really well. Unfortunately, they weren't playing Shelter Cove. They weren't playing with friends who didn't care if Gabriel acted like a child.

They were playing River's Edge. It was the oldest public course in North Platte. From what they'd learned, it was where Big Poppa started playing, when he was a boy about Gabriel's age. They'd been paired with two local boys, Jaybird and TW. Hope thought they were about 15 years older than Gabriel and 10 years younger than her. Jaybird and TW were locked into an ongoing fierce competition with each other that didn't leave them a lot of room for compassion towards Gabriel.

And Gabriel was having a full-on meltdown. There weren't any two ways about that. He'd hit a decent drive on the par 5. He was in great spirits as they walked down off the tee. She'd been talking to TW, who'd grown up on a ranch, about what her mother's life might have been like as a child.

They'd learned that Mom, who she remembered as

Jackie, was actually born Jacquelyn Bismet. Her great-grandfather Charles Bismet, along with his brother Louis, homesteaded adjoining 160 acre quarter sections just north of the confluence of the North Platte and South Platte Rivers right after the Civil War. The next three generations of Bismets flourished and the family transitioned from mixed farming to specialized ranching and cattle breeding. Jackie's grandfather, Henri, was one of the first ranchers in Nebraska to breed Miniature Scottish Highland Cattle, a long-haired dual purpose breed that had become a staple at 4H clubs and county fairs across the Midwest.

Jasper, Jackie's father, was the youngest of Henri's three boys. His two brothers, Jules and Hugo, joined the Navy after Pearl Harbor and were killed at Guadalcanal and Leyte Gulf. Jasper took over the family ranch at 18 after Henri had a nervous breakdown following the war. Jasper kept the business going, adding another quarter section to the family homestead, but only married late in his life, to Esther, who'd worked for him as a cook and housemaid.

TW told Hope that Jasper and Esther would have put Jackie and her sister Paulina to work early and often. "Even miniature cattle crap a lot," he said. "Mucking the pastures and stables would have been a daily chore. Milking, repairing fences—even a small cow will push through just about any fence given enough time—bucking hay bales. Work on the ranch never ends."

"What would they have done for fun?"

"Well," TW told her, "back then they would have been plenty happy to have running water and electricity … TV! You said they did pretty well with their cattle, so they probably had vacations, took trips." He looked at her with as rakish a grin as he could muster. "You know, they say farm girls like to fool around a lot …"

That's when Gabriel hit his second feeble topped fairway wood in a row and lost it. He started screaming and crying and bashed the club against the bottom of his bag a couple of times. He'd never done anything like that at Shelter Cove. He'd only ever had a few epic meltdowns in his whole life. It always happened at the end of a long day like this, after too much excitement.

Hope didn't think bad golf was the main thing that set Gabriel off. Even though she was somewhat older than TW and Jaybird, they were still boys, and she was still a former Ms. Arizona. She didn't have any illusions that bygone farm life was the only thing TW was interested in.

Except for a couple of quick trips to San Francisco, she and Gabriel hadn't really left the extended Shelter Cove/Garberville area since Jason was killed five years ago. Everyone who lived in her community knew that story. Even if they didn't know her, they all knew who she was: the widowed pastor. So Gabriel hadn't had much experience watching males flirt with her, either well or poorly. She was pretty sure he didn't like it very much.

"Gabriel, do you want to skip the rest of this hole or

would you rather play teams from my shot?" They played "teams" sometimes at Shelter Cove, scrambling off their best shot. Gabriel was a pretty good putter and a solid chipper, so his chances of contributing increased as they got closer to the hole.

"NO!" Her son shrieked. "I'm doing it from here!"

"OK," Hope nodded as casually as she could. "Go ahead! I bet you hit this one great!"

"NO!" Gabriel yelled again. "You don't look!"

"OK," Hope replied. She knew it was important to stay calm. The last thing she wanted was to reflect his anger back at him. So she simply stood and watched and waited for him like she would in a normal round at Shelter Cove where these two Nebraska boys weren't shooting nasty looks at her son.

Gabriel took a final, half-hearted slap at the bottom of his bag. He looked at TW, who'd joined Jaybird on the other side of the fairway, about 35 yards ahead of him. He looked back at Hope. She tried to look as bored and uninterested as possible. She glanced up towards her drive and the green.

After a moment, Gabriel seemed satisfied she wasn't paying TW any more attention. He turned and stood over his ball and hit a decent shot about 125 yards up the middle. "Nice shot," she offered in the blandest tone she could muster. What parenting success she'd had with Gabriel, she often credited to erring on the side of doing too little. This family history research trip inspired by his school project had been a bit of an exception to that, at least at the start. Now, after just two days in North Platte, she'd learned so much, she felt the focus of their trip shifting to her. Maybe that was something else Gabriel was upset about.

She watched Jaybird and TW hit their second shots and made her way to her drive, careful to not pay too much attention to anyone. She quickly played down the fairway past the boys, which earned her a quick smile from Gabriel. He was settling down. That was a good time to change the subject.

"Gabriel," she asked, "what do you think your Grandma Jackie would have liked doing growing up on her ranch here in Nebraska?"

Gabriel thought for a moment. "Did they have horses? I bet she would have liked riding horses!" He hit a good iron shot to the front of the green.

"Nice shot! I'm sure they did," Hope agreed. "I bet you're right." They stood back and waited for TW and Jaybird. They both hit the green in regulation and started bragging to each other about the birdies they were going to make. She couldn't really remember much of anything about her mother. Not any conversations they'd had, not any clothes she'd worn, nothing she'd liked to do. She had a vague memory of her face. She associated Mom with warm kitchen smells like soup and fresh pie. That was about it.

"Do you think Grandma would have played with dolls?" Gabriel asked as they approached her ball.

"Maybe." Hope made a good swing with her wedge to about ten feet, good enough for another smile from Gabriel. "It sounds like she had to work a lot. A lot more than you, huh! Maybe we should get some of those miniature cattle?"

Gabriel didn't respond to her teasing as they walked up to the green. Hope left it there as they watched TW and Jaybird miss their birdie putts. Gabriel, to Hope's surprise, stepped up in the midst of their chatter and holed a nice putt from about 25 feet. TW and Jaybird were too wrapped up in negotiating mutually conceded pars to notice. Their match was all square. She hoped it would stay that way. Maybe they'd be more interested in beating each other than talking to her. "Great putt honey!" she told Gabriel. Hope missed her birdie putt, replaced the flag, and they moved on towards the sixteenth, a dogleg par 4.

She looked Gabriel up and down, trying to feel out how tired he was. He smiled back at her. "Do you think Grandma Jackie played golf?"

"Probably not," she told him. "I don't think very many girls played golf back then."

"I wish she could have played with us! Like Grandpa and Uncle BISON playing together." Gabriel let out a peal of laughter. Yesterday they'd had lunch with Jean and

Peggy Pickering, two of Big Poppa's cousins who'd known both her parents "since we were all kids!" They'd shared lots of stories about before and after Jackie and Big Poppa got married. Hope was pretty sure she'd told her son his uncle's name before, but when Peggy mentioned "Bison" for the first time, Gabriel shook with laughter. Now he couldn't say "Bison" without shouting and practically went into hysterics every time he heard the name.

Jean and Peggy called Big Poppa Tommy, for Thomas. Hope had never heard anyone call him Tommy before. They told her how "Tommy" grew up under very different circumstances from his bride-to-be "Jacquelyn." The Bismets were prosperous, successful ranchers. They'd grown their homestead, developed their unique breed of miniature cattle, and kept their family together. People knew who they were and they looked up to them.

The Trombles, on the other hand, were bastards. Literally. Back when that really mattered. People knew who they were and the charitable pitied them. Big Poppa's father Floyd was a rich, powerful man, the Pickerings told her. He'd served for two decades in the unicameral Nebraska Legislature, the smallest state legislature in the country. His wife Gladys kept their stately Victorian mansion on the west edge of downtown immaculately appointed. Her garden parties were the talk of North Platte every spring. Their children went on to great successes of their own.

But Floyd openly kept mistresses. Rachel Tromble, Big Poppa's mother, was the best-known and most longstanding, but there were many others. People called Floyd "the Senator," Jean said. "The Senator ruled North Platte like something out of the old west, or maybe the Bible," she told them. "Even after the war."

The Senator put Rachel and their bastard son Tommy up in a cheap house down by the North Platte, where he'd come visit her when the mood struck him. "Everyone in town knew Tommy was the Senator's son," Peggy said, "but nobody ever talked about it."

What a horrible way to grow up, Hope thought, wondering every night whether your father might be inclined to have his driver bring him by to frolic with your mother. Her heart had gone out to her father even more than ever.

Jaybird tried to skirt the dogleg and pulled his drive left into the trees, much to TW's delight. She saw Gabriel watching them chirp at each other and wondered what he was making of it all. She worried a lot about how he'd learn about men, about being a man. The five years since Jason's murder went by so fast. Gabriel grew up so quick. Hope was constantly scared they'd fallen too far behind for him to ever catch up.

Gabriel was still smiling though, and he hit a good drive down the right side. It rolled out almost to the corner of the fairway, just 50 or 60 yards behind her ball. When everything fell into place, he had such a beautiful swing!

"Do you think you'd like playing golf with Grandpa and Uncle BISON?" she asked as they walked off the tee, imitating the way he screamed Bison's name loudly enough to make Jaybird and TW glance back at them.

"With Uncle BISON!" Gabriel screamed right back with another huge smile. "YES! OK! Not on this trip though," he added in a serious tone.

"No," Hope agreed. "Not on this trip."

"Will they come play at our course?"

"I don't know," Hope told him. "We could ask them. Would you rather play with them there or would you rather go on another trip and play with them somewhere else, somewhere new?"

Gabriel thought about it for a few moments as they approached his ball. He played a mediocre fairway wood that strayed into the right rough. "I wish I could show Grandpa where we live," he started. "But Grandpa says he's going to come visit us and then he never does."

"He does that," Hope nodded. Every year before Big Poppa called for Christmas or on his birthday she sat Gabriel down for a talk. She always explained how Grandpa wanted to visit them, how hurt Grandpa would be if they thought he didn't want to visit them, and how in Grandpa's mind that made it OK to make vague promises about visiting that he probably wouldn't keep. She tried to explain it like Big Poppa was from some foreign country, where they just happened to have different customs that might seem strange to us, but are perfectly normal for them. She hated having to do that.

Hope played her second shot to the left edge of the green and they waited while TW and Jaybird argued about Jaybird's errant drive. "I don't think Bison would do that," she told Gabriel. "I think if he said he was going to come visit, he'd come, unless something bad happened."

"Uncle BISON would come!" Gabriel yelled again, bringing yet another disapproving look from TW.

Hope was really curious to find out how much Bison knew about their parents. Peggy and Jean told her they'd gone to elementary school with both of her parents. They'd known Jacquelyn and Tommy from the time they were kids right up until their divorce. There'd only been about 15,000 people in North Platte back then, they explained. Everyone knew everything about everyone's business.

Jaybird finally took a drop from the trees and played up just short of the green. TW hit a thin shot from the fairway that just managed to hang up on the back of the green. Gabriel strode confidently up to his ball in the rough and popped a well-controlled pitch to the middle of the green. "That's a really good shot!" Hope encouraged him.

"Thanks!" Gabriel replied. His smile turned more serious as he walked to the green and marked his ball.

Hope played her third shot to about two feet and picked up her ball. She watched Gabriel walk back and forth examining his par putt. She could tell this shot had taken on greater meaning than his last, which he'd hit so beautifully. Predictably, he got in his own way a little and pulled his putt left past the hole. "Nice try!" She called. "The rest of that is good."

"NO!" Gabriel yelled, suddenly irked again. It was amazing, Hope thought, how quickly his mood veered up and down. Now, seeing him tense up, bear down, and struggle through his routine, she watched silently, expecting him to fail. To her surprise, he just managed to steer his ball into the hole. He didn't smile though. He just plucked the ball grimly from the hole and turned towards the seventeenth tee. He didn't look like making the putt had been any fun at all. It reminded her of watching Bison golf.

Bison was a little more than nine years older than Hope. She was pretty sure he'd started high school in Phoenix the year after the divorce. So for three or four years before the divorce, Bison would have been older than Gabriel and living with both of their parents in North Platte. He would have seen a lot. He might have seen what went wrong, how their childhood love crumbled.

"Your mom and dad went to high school dances together!" Jean told Hope. "They married young, just a year or two after graduation, like we did back then." Apparently the Bismets tried to turn Big Poppa into a miniature cattle rancher. "Made their first home out on the ranch, but Tommy moved them back to town pretty quick."

"I think it was just a year or two after Bison was born," Peggy added. "He probably doesn't even remember the ranch. They only made a go of it out there for three or four years."

"I don't think your dad was very good at doing one thing very long, at least not when he was young," Jean remarked. Hope thought about the trailer full of meat dryers, golf ball pickers, broken video cameras, and bent old playing cards she'd grown up in. For all she knew, it was all still there in Phoenix. Big Poppa still wasn't very good at doing one thing for very long. He was just the opposite. Big Poppa was great at moving on and starting over. A lot better at that than she was. Hope understood that better now, after learning about Big Poppa's mom and dad.

The seventeenth was a short par 3, wedged tightly between the creek in the middle of the course and the outside of the dogleg on sixteen. They all managed to hit near the green. TW and Hope had manageable birdie putts while Gabriel and Jaybird were just off the green. Jaybird tried to hit a lofted club and skulled his chip. To TW's great amusement, Jaybird's ball rolled out just past his tee shot. Gabriel chipped up and TW resumed his commentary as Jaybird missed badly coming back. TW made a great show of conceding Jaybird's fourth from about four feet before he stepped up, talking the whole time, and stroked in his own twenty-two footer for birdie. Hope watched Gabriel watching Jaybird's head bob up and down as he kept face by telling TW how lucky he was, how things were going to change on the eighteenth. Men, she thought, walked such a fine line between being confident and becoming annoying.

Peggy and Jean told them "nobody really knew" why Tommy and Jackie's marriage fell apart, but Hope had a strong hunch she knew exactly what had happened. For her money, it was that same male dynamic: Big Poppa became annoying by being confident. The Bismets, she was pretty sure, would have felt like they were doing Tommy—the Senator's bastard son—a huge favor by "letting" him marry Jackie and setting them up with a nice ranch home, where they could be part of the family's success and make a "decent" living.

If Hope knew anything about her father though, she knew Big Poppa would never be happy having things done for him. Say what you might, Hope thought, about all of his failed schemes, or businesses, or whatever they were. It took a lot of confidence for Big Poppa to keep believing in his next one as much as he did. Big Poppa was just as much the Senator's son as his half-brothers. The Bismets never would have expected those kids to be grateful for a "decent" ranch life, but they probably felt betrayed when Tommy moved his family back into town: when he tried to build something himself instead of stepping into their family business and being satisfied playing his small part.

The eighteenth tee at River's Edge was perched on the west side of the creek. The hole played back across the creek and over a lake to a green next to the swimming pool, which wouldn't open until after the Fourth of July. It was a pretty hole. Looking down over the driving range, you could see the North Platte peaking through the trees. Hope thought about Big Poppa and Bison standing as children where Gabriel stood now and smiled.

They watched Jaybird hit one of his best drives of the day, which somehow made both him and TW more confident. Hope wondered if Big Poppa ever played here as a child with a friend like that. She and Gabriel teed off. As they walked across the bridge Hope thought about what she'd learned yesterday about her father's childhood friends.

"Sure, sometimes the kids gave Tommy a hard time," Peggy told them after lunch, sitting at one of the picnic tables outside Pizza Gulch, "but it wasn't like everyone picked on him all the time."

"Kids were mean then!" Jean added. "I remember Tommy got in fights."

"All the boys got in fights," Peggy countered. "Jacquelyn wouldn't have gone to dances with Tommy if everyone hated him."

"Do you remember if they ever had best friends? Like in elementary school, before they started dating each other?"

"Jacquelyn had her sister of course," Jean said right away. "Paulina. They called her Pookie, though I can't for the life of me remember why. She was just a year or two older than Jacquelyn. They really stuck together, the two of them, all the time."

"What about Tommy?"

"I'm not sure." Peggy looked at Jean. "It seems weird, but way back in elementary school, more than any of the rest of the boys, I remember Tommy hanging around with his half-brother, the Senator's son!"

Jean nodded. "Yes. I remember that. Tommy and the Judge were good friends at one point, before they all got married."

"Not to each other," Peggy had laughed, seeing Hope's confused look. "You have to remember, this is a small town, and this all was a long time ago! The Senator's son, the Judge, his name was Elihu—it's Welsh—he married Pookie Bismet, your aunt. That would have been, oh I can't remember, it must have been a year or two after Tommy and Jacquelyn got married?"

"So my … half-Uncle … married … my Aunt?"

"Yes," Jean nodded. "Pookie, bless her soul, she was killed, oh it's been five years now I guess. Horrible! An accident at the state fair—she got crushed by one of the rides! And Elihu, he was never a Senator, like his dad, but he was the Judge here for years. He died just recently—

they're saying his second wife killed him!"

"She stabbed him dead in the shower!" Peggy added. "Mercy! Some people say it serves him right, but nobody should die like that!"

Hope played her final iron shot over the pond to the back of the green and two putted. Gabriel laid up safely out to the right away from the pond but hit a poor chip across the green. He hit a good lag putt and Hope scooped up his ball before he could protest. Both TW and Jaybird tried to hit towering aggressive short irons over the pond and bunkers to the front left pin. Jaybird managed to carry the water but left a shot in the bunker before two putting. TW found the water, dropped, hit a better-conceived shot well past the pin and holed another long putt to seal the deal on Jaybird with a scrambling bogey.

Hope and Gabriel shook their hands and listened to Jaybird talk about how much worse he was going to beat TW next time as they all walked past the tenth tee to the parking lot. It felt just like listening to Big Poppa talk about his next can't miss scheme.

Nine: Dougie
Twelfth Tee
Augusta National Golf Club
Augusta, Georgia

"Tobias says this hole plays the most like the real deal," Danny told him. Dougie saw his excitement as he looked out over Rae's Creek. They were standing at the back of the members teeing ground, just slightly above and to the right of the tournament ground. Neither tee was more than 30 or 35 feet long. There just weren't many different places to set the markers. You might have been able to play it from 155 there and only 150 from here. It didn't matter. The green was even narrower and surrounded by peril.

"What did you do yesterday?" With everything else that happened, all he'd learned about the Judge, Dougie hadn't quite processed until this morning that his little brother shot himself a neat little 67 yesterday. Five under his first time around Augusta! Dougie had managed what seemed for a moment like a pretty handy 77. He wasn't surprised that Danny beat him, but ten shots!

"Hit it over the bunker just right of center," Danny replied. "Managed to hold it. Two-putted." Yesterday the pin had been in a relatively forgiving spot just left of center. They'd played it from about 140. Their early tee time let them avoid the swirling mid-afternoon winds. Dougie played a seven iron that went fifteen feet too far left. It ran long and missed the bunker. He'd been glad to get down in four.

Today the tees were further back. It was playing at least 150 and they could feel the breeze swirling back and forth up and down the hills rising from Rae's Creek. The pin was on the far right, near the traditional Sunday spot, where the world fell away from it in every direction. "Nine iron?"

"Wedge," Danny replied. "There wasn't any wind. I wanted to hit something pretty hard, stop it on the green." Dougie, like Dad, had always wondered how great Danny might have been if he'd dedicated his life to competitive golf. It was much breezier today and he was "just" one under. He still had his sweet swing and silky touch, same as ever, and he still seemed to catch every break.

"Longer today. That's probably still the line though, huh? Over the bunker, just right of center?"

"Tobias says that's the line every time, no matter where the pin is, except maybe if it's way left. That's the fattest part of the green, over that bunker, such as it is."

Danny and his caddie Tobias had really hit it off. In the middle of the chaos yesterday, with Kellerman and Pork Chop practically accusing each other of murder, Dougie hadn't really engaged much with his bagman Joe. Today though, playing with Danny and the other New York lawyer, Smiley Postlewaite, things had been more sedate. Dougie told Joe some Bushwood stories and listened to Joe's anecdotes about Augusta, and in particular about

Kellerman. It turned out he was a bit of a folk legend.

"Man sets up over the ball like that," Joe told him as they waited on the sixth, "people gonna talk about him. Don't care if he plays all the time, only plays once, don't matter." Joe grunted deeply and made some deep knee bends, reaching behind himself in a passable imitation of Kellerman's pre-shot contortions. "You can't unsee that! Just natural, folks are gonna wanna know something about the story behind the man who does something like that!"

"He doesn't play a lot," Joe told them walking down the hill to the sixth green, "but everyone who does play a lot, they know the Kellermonkey, that's what they call it. Even if they don't know who he is, don't know anything about him, they all know the Kellermonkey!"

Dougie pulled out his six iron and looked around. He couldn't see anyone on thirteen. The foursome in front of them, who'd been slow all day, was just starting across the Hogan Bridge to the green. He turned and looked back up the hill on eleven, but didn't see any sign of Kellerman and the Bushwood guys. He held his six iron behind him, pumped his knees, and executed a passable Kellermonkey.

Everyone but Postlewaite laughed. Smiley was staring blankly back up the hill towards the clubhouse. He didn't look up. He hadn't exchanged more than a few words with anyone since they teed off. He'd already checked out. He'd done what he needed to do; learned what he needed to learn; said what he'd needed to say:

whatever it was that brought him here, he was over it. He
was ready to go home. Playing golf at Augusta in the April
sunshine with two guys from Nebraska who didn't mean
anything to him was just one last chore.

"I think you could pull it off!" Danny smiled. "Get
distracted, tense up, feel the fear, and flail to fail!" He
laughed. "Huge new instructional video series coming
soon!" Danny grinned up at him with his thousand watt
smile.

Dougie smiled back. He'd watched one of Danny's
instructional videos once. It was impressive, even if he
hadn't followed it all. There was a lot of math involved. It
was a lot better produced than any golf instruction video
he'd seen. Probably because there was so much more
money involved. He'd never been much of a gambler. The
few times he'd been to casinos, mostly on golf trips, he
stuck to simple stuff like sports betting, wagering $5 or $10
on a basketball game he could sit and watch. Danny told
him back on two that twice now, people had watched his
videos and then gone out and won themselves a million
bucks. That didn't happen in golf. You couldn't buy
advertising like that.

Danny still insisted he wasn't a gambler, same as he
always had. He called himself a card player. That all
started when Danny was just a kid, maybe eight or nine.
He and his friends started playing a game with cards of
elves and dragons, where every player collected their own

set of cards. Apparently there was quite a bit of strategy to it. After they'd been playing a couple of years, Danny's friend Steve convinced his parents to drive him and Danny and some of their friends to Omaha to play in the state championship. Steve won. Danny finished in the top ten.

For the next five or six years, as soon as the ground froze and the golf clubs went in storage, Danny played cards just as fervently as he golfed in the summers. Steve actually played in the world championships once, in Canada, when they were 15. He and Danny entered tournaments as far away as Atlanta and Seattle. At one of those tournaments, some of the other kids taught Danny how to play a different kind of card game. A gambling game called Texas Hold-em.

Dougie never forgot the first time Danny got in trouble for gambling and taking other kids' money. He'd told Mom and Dad in his most earnest voice "It's not really gambling! It's just a card game, only you keep score with money." That hadn't gone over so well, at least not at first. But then Danny had explained to Dad how poker tournaments worked just like golf tournaments. Everyone paid their entry fee and the best players cashed out. That clicked with Dad, who'd played golf for money his whole life. After Danny turned 18, he stopped playing with dragons. Soon afterwards, he started winning poker tournaments.

"You're supposed to pick your shot and wait for the

wind, not try to fit the shot to the wind, right?" Dougie flipped his six iron back and forth, looking at Danny as the foursome putted out.

"Or hit while the wind feels wrong, so it's right when the ball's in the air?" Danny smiled back at him. "I think just hit a good shot, execute, let the wind do what it's gonna do."

"That's it!" Tobias chirped in, handing Danny a club. "You just hit a good smooth shot to the fat of that green, we'll maybe roll one in from there, that's all there is to do here." Danny nodded and stepped up between the markers.

Dougie watched him waggle the club back and forth, wiggling his legs into the hallowed ground. Danny was so intuitive. He trusted his instincts in a way Dougie both envied and was terrified of. Dougie couldn't imagine living like that. He always over-prepared for everything. He practiced every chance he got. But somehow everything always worked out so much better for his little brother, just flying by the seat of his pants.

Dougie saw Danny take a final breath as he centered in and let his simple swing send the ball gracefully over the right side of the bunker, where it settled gently on target. "Beautiful!"

"Thanks," Danny smiled. "Lucky with the wind. I don't think it did much of anything."

Dougie stepped up with his six iron. He focused on Danny's ball, relaxed, visualized his ball stopping next to

Danny's, and executed a smooth three-quarter swing. He hit it well, but just couldn't spin it enough to hold the green with a six. It bounced past Danny's ball and gathered a little speed as it rolled down the back of the green. "Nothing wrong with that," Danny encouraged him.

"That's way short of the bunker!" Joe pronounced. "That's gonna be much easier than yesterday," he added, handing Dougie his putter. "Just knock it up and we'll tap it in, we got this!" Dougie nodded to him as Postlewaite stepped up and sent an indifferent mid-iron into the bunker short of the green. The lawyer handed his club to his caddie without comment and strode off towards the Hogan Bridge.

"What about him?" Dougie asked Joe. "He seems like more of a golfer. Does he play with Kellerman a lot? Is he out here a lot?"

"No, don't know that I've seen him with Kellerman before," Joe told them. "Fish there, he usually caddies for him, he's here regular enough for that. He's what the caddies call a working member."

"What's that?" Danny asked as they all started down the hill.

"He don't come for fun," Joe said. "Usually with guests, sometimes meeting other members, but it's always about business, not the golf. Paying people back, cozying up to them. They got rules here about not doing business with your membership …." He laughed. "Don't get me

116

wrong, lot of folks here, most of the really successful ones even, they're exactly the opposite! Just love golf and playing with their friends. They don't wanna talk nothing about *nobody's* business! But there's others, like him and Kellerman. They bring exactly as many guests as they're allowed each year and don't play with the other members so much. They're always here to help themselves out, one way or another, not because they wanna play golf. They might not talk business, but they're doing business just the same."

"And here I thought Smiley was out here having the time of his life with us!" Danny joked. Even before he told Dougie about his 67 yesterday, he'd shared how surreal it had been to stroll around Augusta while Smiley and Stewie Cottleston ignored him and argued about the Judge. To hear Danny tell it, Stewie only went full catering size Sterno, as Pork Chop liked to say, once, on the ninth tee, but their entire round was fraught with tension and suspicion, the two lawyers hardly even pretending to play golf.

Dougie's foursome had been the same, if not worse. Chompers, who maybe loved golf history even more than Dougie, couldn't help being swept away every few minutes by the beauty and grace of this place or by memories of some epic Masters moment that happened "on this exact spot!!" But Pork Chop and Kellerman, they'd locked horns over Judge Smails early and often. As they approached the

Hogan Bridge, Dougie looked back up the hill towards the eleventh tee. He still didn't see their foursome. He hoped they hadn't killed each other.

Smiley led them over the bridge to the green. Dougie watched him walk down into the bunker. From what Danny said, Postlewaite was still 100% convinced Ivanka, the Judge's second wife, murdered him because she was the only one who would have been in the shower with him naked.

Postlewaite wasn't the only one pointing the finger at Ivanka. She wasn't popular at Bushwood, so the Judge didn't bring her around much. Dougie wasn't sure he'd ever had more than a cursory conversation with her. Certainly nothing to make him think she did or didn't do it. But the Judge never told him anything about any fights or disagreements with his young bride, just the opposite in fact. And, Danny told him, Stewie Cottleston had drafted their pre-nup. He'd made sure Ivanka knew exactly how bad it would be if something like this happened to the Judge. Stewie said she was going to lose everything, whether she did it or not.

Dougie had already gathered from listening to Kellerman and Pork Chop that the Judge died in possession of a significant amount of money belonging to the two New York lawyers and the three Bushwood members. None of them knew what the Judge had done with the money. Now the Judge was dead. Supposedly the money couldn't be found. Pork Chop and Kellerman hadn't directly accused each other, but it was clear both suspected the other of being responsible for the missing money and, by extension, the murdered Judge.

Postlewaite bladed his bunker shot over the green towards the thirteenth tee. "That's good for me," he said to nobody in particular, dropping his wedge on the edge of the bunker and walking off across the green towards the tee without waiting for anyone's reaction.

Stewie and Postlewaite had not been as reticent to talk about the missing money around Danny as Chompers and Pork Chop had been with Dougie. Stewie had given Postlewaite an in depth report on the Judge's finances. There was a half-million dollars of their money missing.

Smails had promised them all a payout better than ten to one on that money. Kellerman and Pork Chop, Danny reported, had bit the deepest. They were in for almost forty percent of the action each. They'd expected over two million back! Smiley, Chompers, and Sterno each expected more than a hundred thousand. Now Smails was dead and the money was gone. They'd get nothing and they didn't like it.

Dougie had no idea Pork Chop had that kind of money to invest in the Judge's secret plan. But even more surprising was what else Danny related. "Stewie Cottleston said Smails was a multi-millionaire! Said he owned five or six lumberyards in Minnesota, a bunch of vacation rentals

in Southeast Missouri, some bakery in Omaha. How'd
Smails ever get so rich being a Judge?" Danny asked.
Dougie was shocked. He had no idea. Sure, he'd known
the Judge was a wealthy man, but a multi-millionaire?
He'd never seen any hint of that. Danny said Postlewaite
didn't seem surprised. Said he hadn't asked Cottleston any
questions about the Judge's wealth except how they were
going to extract their five million, or at least their original
half-million, from it.

Dougie walked across the green and saw his ball was
in a good position. It came to rest at the very bottom of the
little valley between the green and the back bunkers. He'd
seen this shot hundreds of times. It needed to crest the hill
with just enough speed to trickle out towards the hole,
where it would break ever so slightly to the right, but not
enough speed to risk tumbling down the other side into
Rae's Creek. He focused on the crest of the hill, relaxed by
wiggling his legs like Danny on the tee, trying to feel his
brother's energy, visualized the ball trickling to the hole,
and executed his stroke.

"That's right!" Dougie heard Joe say as the ball was
still rolling up the hill. He stood up and watched the ball
carry just enough speed over the top to trundle calmly
across the green and cozy up about six inches short of the
hole.

"Great shot!" Danny chimed in.

"Don't get much better than that" Tobias added.

"Thanks!" Dougie smiled as Danny walked over and knocked his ball back to him. Dougie caught it with his putter and flipped it up into his pocket.

Walking up the hill on nine today, after Danny told him about the Judge's wealth, Dougie realized his question—why didn't the Judge live like a multi-millionaire?—was inextricably bound to Danny's question—how did the Judge accumulate so much wealth? Neither of them knew how much the State of Nebraska paid its Judges, but both of them knew it wasn't enough to buy lumberyards, lake cottages, or bakeries in Omaha. However the Judge got rich, Dougie thought, it wasn't something he wanted people yapping about. It certainly wasn't modesty that kept the Judge from flaunting his wealth.

"Might have been one big score a long time ago," Danny had speculated back on nine, "and he just played his cards right from there. Money makes money." Danny had stopped and given him a serious look. "People scoff at Marx these days, but his general formula of capital— monetizing wealth creates surplus value to accumulate profits without contributing your own labor—that's spot on." They'd been standing just in front of the ninth green, watching Postlewaite chip up the hill towards the historic clubhouse. "Heck," Danny said with a smile, "that's basically what I do now!"

Dougie watched Danny stalk his nineteen-foot birdie

putt and smiled. Danny told him last night he'd been doing a lot of reading and sitting in on classes at different colleges. "I just go sit in the back—nobody cares! Catching up on some of the things I might have missed out learning about at college." It wasn't until the eleventh tee today, asking Danny about some to the classes he'd visited, that Dougie realized it was as close as he'd ever heard Danny come to talking about Mom, about everything that happened after she died.

It was so long ago now Dougie didn't think about her much. Today though, playing golf with Danny for the first time in so many years, Mom was on his mind plenty. They couldn't do much about cancer back then. She died pretty quick, not even three months after she first got sick. In some ways, Dougie thought, she suffered as little as any of them.

Dad took the worst of it, of course. He might have lived another fifteen years before his body finally gave out, but his heart died right there with Mom. Dougie remembered Heidi telling him when they had Belinda, their first daughter, that having a grandchild would be good for Dad, would give him something to live for. Dad loved Belinda. He doted on her, on all their daughters, every chance he got, as much as he could. But his heart just wasn't ever there again.

Dougie started dating Heidi about a year before Mom passed. They got engaged right before she got sick, so it was something they'd gone through together. Like everything else, Heidi made it so much easier on him. She was the strongest person he'd ever met. Dougie still couldn't believe she married him. They'd postponed their wedding for a year, and then over the next few years Dougie took the head pro job, they had Belinda, and he got so busy with everything. He just ran out of time to be distraught.

But Danny's life probably changed more than anyone's. Before Mom got sick, he'd aced his SAT (without studying, of course) and walked away with the state high school championship at Bushwood his senior year. He'd been recruited by some of the best college golf programs in the country. Famous coaches came to North Platte and promised Danny and Dad the best preparation for the PGA Tour career everyone assumed he dreamt of. Even as a kid though, Danny always danced to his own beat. He wrote school newspaper articles and performed in school plays as enthusiastically as he played golf or cards. He'd wound up picking Yale. "The best school with the best golf course," he told them.

Mom was so proud. Then, just a couple of weeks later, she got sick. Danny went into a tailspin. He managed to get through graduation, barely. But he never made any plan to move back East to New Haven and start school. How could he plan on leaving his dying mother? And it's not like Dougie or Dad been much help. They'd been so wrapped up with Mom and so occupied with their own issues.

Now, watching Danny look over his birdie putt one last time, for the first time in a long time Dougie felt really bad about not doing more for his little brother back then. It had all happened so fast. Mom died. Danny didn't go to New Haven. He left North Platte suddenly, they didn't know exactly where he was for a while, and then, because he was Danny, he turned up in Las Vegas sitting on a pile of cash after winning a big poker tournament. But just because everything always came up roses didn't mean Danny hadn't been through some shit.

Danny's timing, as always, was impeccable. Cable networks were just starting to broadcast poker tournaments. More people were starting to play. After they gave him the money, one of the players Danny had eliminated, a guy from La Jolla who'd been in corporate video production, asked him to be in an instructional video, talking about Texas Hold-em strategy. Instead of money, Danny convinced Phil to give him a piece of the new poker video company. Poker kept growing, Danny kept winning, the video company kept expanding, and Danny's checks kept getting bigger and bigger.

Now, almost thirty years later, Danny told him he'd invested all his money back into so many different businesses he needed a full-time accountant to keep track of it all. These days, Danny told him last night, he only played poker tournaments for charity: partnering with different organizations and donating anything he won, trying to promote awareness for different causes.

Danny drew back his vintage Ping Anser, the same putter he'd used as a kid, and stroked smoothly through the ball, his body perfectly still and balanced. Dougie watched his ball track flawlessly across the green, drifting ever-so-gently right, and settle neatly into the middle of the hole. "That's a putt, right there!" Tobias said.

"Great putt!" Joe agreed.

"Fantastic birdie!" Dougie added.

Danny plucked his ball from the hole and smiled. "That felt pretty darn good!" He tossed the ball to Tobias and they all started walking down towards the next tee, which sat on the bank of Rae's Creek next to the Nelson Bridge.

"So what do you think?" Danny asked him. "Could any of these guys really have killed Judge Smails?"

Dougie looked at Postlewaite waiting on the tee. He looked back up the hill, but still didn't see Kellerman or Pork Chop. "I don't know," he admitted. "I feel bad even thinking about it."

"The moment you found out he was dead," Danny asked, "did you have any immediate reaction? Did you think about his wife right away?"

"No, not at all," Dougie told him. "Just the opposite! I assumed it was some criminal he'd sentenced, something

like that. Somebody I didn't know. Somebody who didn't
have anything to do with me!"

"But now?"

"I just don't know." Dougie shook his head. "I
thought coming here, crazy as it sounds, would have got
us—got me—further away from the Judge's murder, not
plunged us right into the middle of it all!"

Ten: Bison
Eighteenth Green
Golf Club of Houston – Tournament Course
Humble, Texas

Bison had never seen anyone so pissed off over a four-inch tap in for a bogey-free 68. But Merritt hadn't made a single putt of consequence today. He'd missed several easy ones. He was about to miss the cut by two despite rebounding brilliantly from his 76 yesterday. His second shot on this challenging par 4, a towering five iron from just over 200 yards, couldn't have missed the pin by more than a few inches. That's how Merritt hit the ball all day. He'd missed one green, on eleven, where he'd hit a marvelous bunker shot inside two feet. He could easily have shot 58 or 59. 62 or 63 should have been automatic. But he just couldn't sink any putts. And he kept getting angrier and angrier.

Merritt's face was trembling as he marched to the hole, shaking his putter up and down. "By God," he snarled, "somebody's gonna pay for this!" Bison could see the tension in his hands. He tried to remember if he'd ever seen anyone so angry on a golf course. It certainly wasn't anything he'd seen from Merritt before. Usually he was totally wrapped up in his own game—too self-absorbed with his fidgeting to let anything external throw him off even a little, much less melt him down like this.

Bison couldn't remember ever seeing Merritt hit any shot without going through his routine. Not in practice, and certainly not on the course. So when Merritt stabbed his ball furiously into the hole without any preparation, Bison knew his anger was out of control.

Merritt didn't reach down or take his ball out of the cup. He straightened up. Turning slowly, he pointed in turn at Sukert, his caddie Ryan, Bison, and Hamilton. "I'll see you in the scoring tent," he told them ominously. "All of you!" Leaving his ball in the cup, Merritt tossed his putter in the direction of his bag without looking and stalked away towards the clubhouse. Bison saw Dodger, Merritt's caddie, shaking his head as he walked over to retrieve the putter.

"No problem," Hamilton, of all people, replied. Bison looked up in surprise and saw his caddie hustling to the hole. He retrieved Merritt's ball and rolled in neatly to Dodger. "OK," Hamilton nodded to Sukert, "knock this in and let's get on with it!"

Sukert stood silently in the middle of the green taking it all in. He'd played well, made a few putts, and was safely under the cut line. The fresh-faced southerner watched and waited as Dodger picked up Merritt's bag and started towards the clubhouse. "Best o'luck to y' both on t' weekend," he nodded politely to Bison and Sukert.

"Thanks Dodger. Best of luck to you as well," Bison said. Sukert nodded back and started looking over his putt, a two foot formality to end their day.

"Thanks Dodger," Hamilton added, but the old Scot

was already around the corner and didn't look back.

Bison looked back down the fairway and saw the group behind them waiting. "OK," he heard Hamilton say, "one more putt and we're on to the weekend!" He and Sukert both looked up, taken aback by Hamilton's sudden verbosity.

"Don't worry about him," Ryan interjected, shooting Hamilton a look. He walked up and pointed to a spot well left of Sukert's line. "This ridge over here isn't going to do anything." He walked back up and around Sukert's putt. "It's just outside right and you're going to snap it right into the back of the cup."

It was a lot of information for a two foot putt, but Ryan's words had the desired effect. Sukert stopped thinking about Merritt, or Hamilton, and focused on his putt. After a few practice strokes, he put a good roll on it and they heard it click off the back into the cup. "OK!" Ryan congratulated him. "That's a good finish! Great round!"

Bison walked up and stuck out his hand. "That was a good finish," he said. "Congratulations! Good luck this weekend. Hope we get to play again sometime."

Sukert smiled and shook his hand. "Thanks! You too." His face grew more serious. "What did he mean, somebody's going to pay? What was he talking about?"

"If I understood how Merritt thinks," Bison told him, "I'd be writing psychology textbooks for some rich university, not out here trying to play golf. He's just pissed off about playing bad yesterday and then putting so bad today, hitting it like that."

"I hope so," Sukert said as they walked to the side of the green and handed their putters to Ryan and Hamilton. "Pretty sure I haven't seen anyone get their shorts wound that tight since junior golf."

"Great round!" Bison saw Big Poppa standing behind the green smiling. He'd disappeared from their gallery somewhere around sixteen, but in between dealing with Merritt and finishing his own round, Bison hadn't thought much about it.

Bison wasn't sure where Big Poppa had got off to—it looked like he'd just walked down from the clubhouse— but he waved his hat back to him and smiled. "Not bad, huh Dad?"

"Really good!" Big Poppa smiled. "Two days to go!" Once again, his elderly father spun around in a distorted little dance that made Bison smile and then cringe a little.

"We've got to go sign the cards," Hamilton interrupted them. He reached into their bag and pulled out the keys to the Land Rover. "Why don't you," he nodded at Big Poppa, "go and get the car? We'll meet you in front of the clubhouse in about 10 minutes."

Big Poppa stopped twirling and looked at Hamilton. After a moment, Big Poppa stepped forward and took the keys. "OK. Want me to take the bag too?"

"Let's leave the bag here tonight," Bison interjected. "I want to enjoy this, for a few hours at least. We'll start up again tomorrow."

"Sounds good," Hamilton nodded. He shot them a confident look. "Guess it's time to see what he thinks somebody needs to pay for!"

Bison stared at the bespectacled teenager. He looked just like the quiet kid who'd carried his bag in the qualifier at Cypresswood on Monday. But he sure didn't sound or act much like him. In just five days, he'd gone from nervously silent to aggressively competent. Maybe even overconfident. If he'd improved his game as much as Hamilton had improved his caddying, they'd have shot 54 today, no problem.

"I guess," Bison replied, trying to downplay the situation. Merritt had been out here a long time. He was just angry, and mostly with himself. He'd calm down soon enough. They just needed to give him time. "I've got the card." He retrieved his valuables from the pouch pocket, opened his wallet, and handed Hamilton fifty bucks. "You take this down to the bag room and check us in while Big Poppa gets the car. Take care of them down there! I'll deal with Merritt, sign the cards, skip the locker room, meet you two out front. We'll clean up at the hotel, have a nice dinner." Hamilton's new-found confidence made him uncomfortably unpredictable. It might spur him to say something unfortunate. Better to let Merritt squawk out his anger and stay silent so they could all move on.

"But he said he wanted us all there!" Hamilton objected. "He pointed at me!"

Bison didn't say anything right away. He stared at Hamilton for a moment and gave Big Poppa a more pointed look. This kid was his doing. "He doesn't make the rules," Bison told Hamilton calmly. "There's no rule says caddies have to be there to add up scores and sign cards."

"But caddies do have to do what they're told!" Big Poppa added. He shot a stern glance at Hamilton. "Maybe you haven't read enough about that part of it yet!" He slapped their bag with his cane. "C'mon now, pick it up! I'll go down to the bag room with you, make sure they know whose bag this is, we'll go get the car." He smiled at Bison. "Maybe you get out of the clubhouse before us, sign a few autographs, see if there's any friendly young women up there trying to meet a champion golfer!"

"Sure Poppa," Bison smiled. "If there are, I'll tell them all about you."

"OK," Hamilton said. "We'll go check the bag in." He gave Bison a determined look. "But you have any trouble with Merritt, you just send for us." Bison nodded as seriously as he could, wondering who this kid was, who he'd become. Hamilton finally picked up the bag and headed towards the bag room with Big Poppa. As they turned the corner, Bison saw Big Poppa start playfully tapping the bill of Hamilton's cap with his cane.

Bison shook his head. He was pretty sure nobody else in the field had an entourage like his. Tonight, he decided, he'd either get Hamilton's full story or consider changing caddies for the weekend. Dodger wasn't making any money with Merritt. He'd looked chuffed by his outburst. Maybe he'd be game for a new bag. Dodger was a solid caddie, a real pro who'd never be a distraction.

Bison was surprised to find seven or eight kids waiting along the clubhouse path with markers and oversized balls. They'd started late and there were only a couple of groups left on the course. He took his time, trying to get the kids to talk about golf. He wrote something personal on each ball, and signed his name carefully. One time his friend Hunter Haas spent a few extra minutes talking to a kid and wound up giving the kid a wedge he was sick of. Turned out the kid's dad was on the tournament board. Hunter played there every year after that, whether he was eligible or not. Bison always tried to make extra time for kids.

After he signed the last ball and thanked the kids, he continued up the path and saw Sukert coming out of the scoring tent. Ryan was standing there with their bag. "He's going ballistic," Zach informed them, shaking his head.

"About what," Bison asked. "We didn't putt for him." Ryan let out a chuckle at that.

Sukert smiled. He shook his head again. "I wouldn't

know where to start. They just now asked me to go find you. Where's Hamilton?"

"I was signing autographs for those kids," Bison told him. "I'd like to see them give me a hard time about that. Hamilton's checking our bag in."

He followed them back into the scoring tent. Merritt was standing at one end of the table shaking his fingers at two rules officials. "… something to make me fall apart," he shouted at them. "Doing something to mess with my emotions! It was something hidden in his bag, or maybe on his caddie! His caddie said I was still away! They messed with me!"

"OK John, let's just be sure we talk through what happened out there before anybody accuses anyone of anything."

"I'm not accusing them. I'm telling you what they did!" Merritt shot a withering glance at Sukert. "His caddie belittled me, yesterday, on our very first hole! Then they did something to me … something to make me angry and put me off my game!"

"Off your game?" Sukert replied. "That was one of the best rounds I've seen! You shot 68! If that was off your game, I can't imagine what it looks like when you're on form!" He shook his head.

"Today: the putting," Merritt growled. "Yesterday: everything! From the very first hole! He thought I couldn't hear him from the bunker, so your caddie, what does he say: 'you're still away!'" Merritt shook his fist and stared at Ryan. "I don't know how you did it," he glared at Sukert, "but I know what you did!" He looked around. "Where's the other one, your kid?" He glared at Bison.

Bison sat down and flattened his scorecard on the table. "That was as tough a day as I've seen anyone have on a golf course in a long time John," he told Merritt with as much sympathy as he could muster. "Never seen you hit the ball like that. Never seen anyone hit the ball like that. Maybe Tiger, the Open at Pebble. Every shot you hit today was absolutely gorgeous except your wedge on eleven. And that wasn't really a bad shot, just about fifteen feet left. It didn't hold like it should have, rolled out into the bunker. That was unlucky as much as anything."

"I've never putted like that!" Merritt challenged him. "How do you explain that!"

"You putted bad," Bison acknowledged. "Today. But yesterday you made some putts. How do you explain that? You're saying Sukert and Ryan laid some sort of heebie jeebie curse on you, all it did was mess up your putting today, when you hit the ball so great, but yesterday it messed up your swing, but not your putting stroke?"

"I don't know!" Merritt shouted. Bison hoped his praise would calm him down. It didn't seem to be working. "I told you," he pointed at the rules officials, "I don't know how they did it, but I know what they did! They did something to scramble my nerves, make me miss all those putts!"

Sukert shook his head. He sat down and set his scorecard on the table. "That's just crackers," he told Merritt. "You're saying I cheated to make you shoot 68? What sense does that even make?"

"Mr. Merritt has not formally accused anyone of anything," the older rules official interjected hastily. Bison knew from experience the last thing either of them wanted was for anything official to develop from this.

"John, I can't say you're my best friend out here," Bison told him. "But I respect you. I've never heard anyone say you were anything but a straight-shooter, a guy who calls it like he sees it. You think you were interfered with, my money says you're telling the truth." He paused.

"But," Merritt said with a scowl.

"But," Bison told him calmly, "think for a second about the big picture here. Maybe you're not gonna do yourself any favors making some official complaint about them doing something, you don't know what, that made you putt so bad you shot 68?" He looked at Merritt. "Let's just sit here a minute, go over all our numbers, you think for a moment about what it might be like for the rest of your career, answering questions about when you accused Zach Sukert of cheating by mind control. Try to imagine when you win another tournament, you got to go answer questions about something like that!"

Merritt didn't say anything, but he put his card on the

table and sat down. "OK Tromble," he nodded, "you've got a point there." Merritt settled down long enough to read out Bison's scores, three holes at a time. Bison did the same for Sukert's, and Zach finished with Merritt's. They all agreed, and after an uncomfortable moment of silence Merritt scribbled his name on Bison's card, reached across and grabbed his card from Sukert, signed it quickly, and stood up. "You got away with it this time," he pointed at Sukert and Ryan, who thankfully kept his head down. "But I'm watching out for you!" Merritt stormed out of the tent.

"Thank you," the rules officials told Bison. "Thank you very much!"

"Takes all kinds," Bison told them. He looked at Sukert. "Next time you guys curse somebody, at least make them shoot over par!" He tried to laugh, but nobody had any energy for it. Merritt's outburst had drained them all. Bison had been on top of the world all day, but now, after this, he just wanted to crawl into bed. Suddenly playing this weekend sounded a lot less exciting.

"You fellows don't worry about him," the older rules official told them. "Get a good night's sleep, forget about all this. Good luck on the weekend!"

They thanked them, shook hands, and left the scoring tent. The last two groups of the day were waiting with quizzical looks. Bison was sure word would get out soon enough. There weren't a lot of secrets on tour and they'd probably heard the shouting. But right now, he just wanted to go find Big Poppa and Hamilton and get out of here. "Well," he told Sukert, "that's good advice. Let's forget this and move forward with the weekend!" They shook hands again and wished each other luck.

Shaking his head as he walked up the clubhouse path, Bison tried to figure out what in the world Merritt was talking about. That incident on ten yesterday, where Sukert hit that great bunker shot after their back and forth and then Merritt putted it outside him, hadn't seemed like that big a deal. They'd boiled over on the eleventh tee, but the rest of the round had been pretty uneventful. Today the two of them hadn't gotten into it at all. But apparently Merritt had just kept boiling the whole time. It wasn't like him, paying that much attention to his surroundings. None of it made any sense.

Thankfully, the parking lot was clear and they were waiting for him. He climbed in and Hamilton pulled away. "What'd he say?" the teenager asked.

"He said Sukert and Ryan did something … somehow they scrambled his nerves!" Bison told them. "He said the reason he missed all those putts today, the reason he played bad yesterday, was some kind of mojo curse they put on him. I don't know what the hell he was talking about."

"Curse?" Big Poppa asked from the back.

"That's what he said," Bison nodded. "I don't know. He seemed pretty convinced. I've played with him enough times … this just isn't like him at all. He's always so wrapped up in his own world. Usually people complain he doesn't pay enough attention to them, now he's paying so much attention to Sukert he's out of his mind?"

"He putted OK yesterday though, didn't he?"

"Yep," Bison agreed. "Not great, but nothing like today."

"What did Sukert say?" Hamilton asked as he merged the Pathfinder onto the Sam Jackson and they headed downtown.

"He had no idea what he was talking about. Neither did Ryan. Thought he'd lost his mind."

Big Poppa pulled himself up between the seats. "So how did it end? Did he file some kind of complaint?"

"No. I told him to think about winning another tournament and having to answer questions about something like that. He's not stupid. He didn't go away happy, but he went away."

"Good," Hamilton chirped, banging his hand against the wheel. Bison didn't know quite what to make of that, so he leaned back and let it go. Enough about Merritt. He needed to figure this kid out and get focused on the weekend. He was still in contention, just five shots back of the leaders.

Going against traffic, it didn't take them long to get to the hotel. "OK," Bison told them as they left the garage, "we're gonna meet in the lobby in 20 minutes, go get dinner, get our heads right, ready for the weekend." The top guys, guys who made eight out of ten cuts, Friday nights weren't any big deal for them. But guys like Bison, who missed more cuts than they made, had to balance acknowledging their success with not letting down or feeling like their job was done. Friday nights were for refocusing on what he needed to do and preparing to finish like a champion.

After he showered, Bison decided he wanted to stay close to the hotel and forgo anything fancy. He went down to the lobby and the bellhop recommended Frank's Pizza a few blocks away in Market Square. Hamilton and Big Poppa showed up. They walked around the parking garage and found a reasonably quiet table. Big Poppa handed Hamilton a $100 bill and told him to go order for them.

Once he'd gone, Bison turned and focused squarely on Big Poppa. "OK Poppa, what the hell is the story with this kid?"

Big Poppa sputtered something about "signs of promise as a caddie" but Bison cut him off.

"That's not what I mean. Who is he, where did you meet him, and why is he here?"

"I don't know what you …"

"Cut it out Poppa. You didn't find him in the parking lot. What's going on?"

Big Poppa fidgeted around a little more. He let out a big sigh. "Well, I guess you had to find out eventually."

"Find out what?"

"He's the son of my business partner, Elijah Montgomery. Elijah, he's brilliant! Son, he understands this world in a way that is just flat beyond most people. He's not a vain man, he doesn't promote himself. Nobody has ever heard of him! But the things he's figured out …." Big Poppa bent down towards Bison. "He can't reveal it all at once, you understand. The whole world would go crazy!"

"So why's his son here with you?" Bison leaned back and tried to hide his disappointment. He should have known. It was just another one of Big Poppa's crazy schemes. The thing with Merritt already had him down. He'd tried to rally, but now this. Just when he'd started thinking it would be fun having Big Poppa around for a while.

Big Poppa picked up his big silver cane and handed it across the table. "It's called the magnustifier!" Big Poppa smiled. "It's gonna change the world, and we've got the only one!!" Bison reached out and just about dropped the cane. It was heavy.

"What's in this thing?"

"Don't have the first clue, Son, but that right there, that's the reason you're gonna win this tournament! Then you're gonna go win the Masters!" He broke into a somewhat restrained seated version of his happy dance.

"What are you talking about!?!" Bison shook the staff. Whatever it was, it was seriously heavy. He looked at Big Poppa, wondering as much as anything how he'd dragged this thing around for 36 holes.

"What are you doing!?!" Bison looked up and saw Hamilton, his face distraught. "Why did you show that to him? You've ruined everything!!"

Eleven: Hope
Ninth Tee
River's Edge Golf Club
North Platte, Nebraska

Gabriel's smile made their whole trip worthwhile. He could hardly stand still, rocking back and forth and fidgeting with his bag. Hope couldn't remember the last time she'd seen him so happy. He'd just made the first birdie of his life. Whatever else they'd accomplished here, she was pretty sure he'd be joining her at Shelter Cove a lot more after this.

"Gabriel, go ahead!" Dylan called to them from the blue tees. "Your honors, birdie man!"

Gabriel looked up at Hope. "It's a Fuddie Duddie rule," she explained. "The person who makes the lowest score on a hole has the 'honor' and hits first on the next tee." That's what they called golf rules that weren't common sense, like the differences between red stakes, yellow stakes, and white stakes. Winter storms stripped all the paint off most of the stakes at Shelter Cove long ago: only a Fuddie Duddie would worry about what color they used to be. "Go ahead!"

"OK!" Gabriel grabbed his driver and strode confidently to the tee. Eight and nine were two of the most challenging holes at River's Edge. Both demanded forced carries over water, on the approach to this par 4 and for the second at the par 5 eighth. Gabriel hit one of his best drives ever on eight, followed up with a solid three wood, and stuck a wedge from 85 yards to about fifteen feet.

Hope watched him step in and, flush with excitement, swing a lot faster and harder than he had on eight. Predictably, he came over the top and pull-hooked it down the left side through the row of trees lining the fairway towards the access road that ran out across the creek through the open space between nine and sixteen. "OK," she encouraged him, "I think there's some room out there!"

"No problem Champ!" Dylan yelled from behind them. "I think it stopped on the road! Buy you an ice cream cone if you make another birdie from there!"

"OK!" Gabriel yelled back, still smiling despite his poor shot. "But I get a double cone for two birdies!"

"You got it!" Dylan smiled back as Hope laughed. She motioned for Dylan to go. He was a good player, with a smooth swing and relaxed attitude that reminded her of Peter. He was also really nice. She was glad he was the first bona fide relative they'd met here. She was glad they were playing golf with him.

Dylan was Big Poppa's half-grandnephew and Mom's grandnephew-in-law. They'd met by chance at the courthouse yesterday. His mother, Gwen, was the daughter of Big Poppa's half-brother, Elihu Smails, who Dylan called Judge Smails, and Mom's sister Paulina, who Dylan called Grandma Pookie. Dylan grew up in Missouri, where Gwen managed property rentals, but he lived in New York City. He was a staff attorney for the Anti-Violence Project, providing free legal services for gay, lesbian, bi, trans, and queer survivors of violent crimes and domestic abuse. He'd come to North Platte—"the last place I ever thought I'd go again"—just last week, to watch over the handling of his grandfather's estate on Gwen's behalf.

"And I'm sure he's been rolling over in his grave ever since I got here and started poking through his business!" Dylan had told her. Judge Smails hadn't treated Dylan very well after he started being open about his sexuality. He didn't see or speak with his grandparents for years before they died. His mother Gwen hadn't been particularly supportive either. She'd refused to visit him in New York, or to allow his boyfriends to come home to Missouri with him. "But now that she needs a good lawyer," he'd laughed, "suddenly none of that matters quite so much!" Dylan had been looking through some of the Judge's old papers yesterday when Hope and Gabriel went to see the office of Big Poppa's half-brother and childhood friend. They'd gotten to talking, discovered a mutual connection to River's Edge, and agreed to meet for golf.

Dylan knocked a solid drive down the middle of the fairway. He'd played golf just about every day he'd been in North Platte. "There's not really any legal work on the Judge's estate right now," he'd explained earlier. "Mostly it's just going through all his papers and records. Trying to figure out everything he owned, making sure nothing goes missing—or gets hidden. He had an accountant and a lawyer—his lawyer gets back in town this evening. He was in Georgia. Playing Augusta! Judge Smails was supposed to go. He got murdered and his lawyer went ahead and went golfing at Augusta without him!" He'd shaken his head and chuckled. "That's our family! Anyway, Mom doesn't trust either of them one bit. She begged and pleaded until I agreed to come out and keep an eye on things, look out for her inheritance."

Hope teed her ball low and played a smooth three-wood down the middle that stopped well short of the hazard. "Great shot Mom!" Gabriel was still smiling as Dylan caught up with them and they started down the fairway. Driving into the trees hadn't fazed Gabriel at all. He was doing so much better with Dylan than he had with TW and Jaybird, Hope thought, even though Dylan was around their same age.

Gabriel ran over to the left side of the fairway and started stomping around the trees looking for balls. "Double scoop for two birdies!" he reminded Dylan, who laughed again.

"He's my second cousin, or third cousin, or something like that, right? He's my favorite cousin! He's a great kid!"

"Thanks," Hope smiled. "He's been through a lot."

"You said his dad Jason passed away?"

"Murdered," Hope nodded. "It's been about five years now."

"I'm sorry! Does talking about it make you uncomfortable?" Dylan looked at her. "We work with people whose loved ones were taken from them. Believe me, I get not wanting to think about it, much less talk about it."

"Yes and no," Hope told him. "Like I said, we live in a pretty small town, just a few thousand people, in a pretty insular part of the world. Everyone there, they already know pretty much the whole story as far as who Jason was, what happened, and so on. So there's not really any reason for people to talk about it. I never talk about it. If somebody heard someone ask me about Jason, people would start talking about why that person was asking, not about Jason, or me, if that makes any sense."

"Sure," Dylan nodded. "The queer community can be like that, even in a big city like New York. Did you have to sit through the trial?"

"No," Hope said. "There was no trial. Ted … the one who killed Jason. He got killed by … somebody else." She paused. "One of Jason's brothers, or a cousin … they killed Ted. Jason's family killed Ted. I don't know exactly who did it, but it was Jason's family. They grow marijuana. Ted shot Jason by mistake, thinking he was his brother Jeff. Ted and Jeff were part of some drug deal gone bad …."

"I'm so sorry!" Dylan interrupted. He looked over at Gabriel. "I think it's just past that next tree, Champ, on the road there, maybe right next to it!" He pointed. "Is it hard to stay there and keep seeing all those people?" He looked back at Hope. "Do you ever think about relocating, getting away from there, starting over somewhere else?"

"Not really," Hope said. "Jason's family—they're pretty close-knit." She looked over at Gabriel. He'd found his drive on the edge of the access road and was looking at it. "Move it off the road so you don't hurt your club!" He nodded and kicked his ball to a grassy area.

"And it's strange," she told Dylan, "but I don't think I could leave the church! I never thought of myself as a religious person. Not at all! When Jason's family set up the church for me, after he died, it was really just a tax thing, at least at first. They could donate cash to the church, and I could use the money to take care of Gabriel and myself. It was all very nice and legal once they gave their drug money to the church."

"But now?" They watched Gabriel take a mighty swing from the edge of the access road with what looked like his hybrid. He hit another great shot! Hope watched it fly over the hazard and roll out under one of the trees on the right side of the green bordering the driving range. "Good one!" She yelled.

"I'm going to make that one!" Gabriel shouted back.

"Of course you are! Nice shot!" Dylan chimed in. Gabriel waved his club in the air and jumped up and down. Hope could see his smile from across the fairway.

"Now?" she laughed. "Now I love it! Sometimes I wonder what God must think about our strange little church. But what I feel in my heart, what my divine spark tells me, is that we're doing great things!" Hope stopped at her drive and put down her bag. "I don't know if we've saved any souls, but we help out a lot of people who are in tough spots. We find a lot of joy in just working together, being a community."

"That's fantastic!" Dylan nodded. "Somebody asked me about preachers once," he continued as Hope took out her five iron. He waited while she played safely across the hazard and just short of the green. "Nice shot! I told them I meet two kinds of preachers. The ones who help people with their problems are some of the best people I've ever met. The ones who save people's souls can be some of the worst."

Hope smiled and wiped her club. "I don't like to talk bad about anyone … but I know just what you mean." She picked up her bag. "When our church first opened, some of the local preachers were really hostile, said bad things about us. We stuck it out!"

"And now?"

"Now they probably still say bad things about us, but at least they have to be more discrete about it!" They both laughed as they walked up to Dylan's drive.

Dylan put his bag down. His ball was about 35 yards short of the hazard. He only had a wedge left. "What about the rest of your family?" he asked. "Are all my newfound relatives as cool and fun as you and Gabriel?"

Hope laughed. "I'm too old to be cool and fun. Gabriel's too young not to be." She paused for a second. "I guess you'll probably get to see for yourself. Like I said, it's just me, my dad, and my brother. I finally got in touch with my brother last night, at his apartment in Dallas. Dad was there with him. Apparently they're on their way here right now! They're driving to North Platte!"

"To see you?"

"No, like I said, I haven't seen either of them in a long, long time. They had no idea we were here! It's some business deal my dad's involved in, something about golf—that's why Bison's involved. Probably something shady—that's how my dad works." Hope paused for a second. "It's strange though. I told you about Gabriel's school project, on his family history?"

"And how it led you here, to learn more about your family … about our family."

"Right! Our spring break family history trip! I thought perhaps, after this, maybe this summer, we'd visit Dad, or see Bison. But now they're on their way here! Both of them!" Hope shook her head. "I don't think we've all been together since Gabriel was born! It's just a lot happening at once." She shook her head again. "It will be fun—maybe we can all play golf!" Hope shook her head a third time. "What about the rest of your family—our family? Are the rest of them all sending their own brilliant young lawyers to North Platte?"

"I don't think so," Dylan smiled. "Unless somebody from the Judge's second wife's family shows up. I hope they will! Ivanka's in a bad spot."

"Because she killed him?"

"That's what everyone seems to think. Have you met her? We had coffee a few days ago. She's not what I expected. Not at all."

"And? Do you think she did it?"

"No. No, I don't. Not because she says she didn't— they all say that, at least in my limited experience. But she seems smart enough to know she'd never get away with it. Not in North Platte. And she's plenty savvy enough to understand that if she did kill him her best move would be to argue self-defense—battered woman syndrome." Dylan chuckled. "Judge Smails was a pig. Every woman in Western Nebraska knew that."

"You think he abused her?"

"No, probably not by North Platte standards he didn't. But he was a rich old bastard who only cared about himself. I'm sure he disrespected her plenty, did enough stupid and embarrassing stuff that, if she did kill him, there'd be evidence enough to argue abuse." Dylan waggled his wedge a few times. He settled over the ball and made another smooth swing. The ball shot into the air with a crack. It looked like it was going to hit the flag! It flew right over the hole and settled on the back of the green, ten yards too far.

"Bet you an ice cream cone you don't make it from there!" Gabriel called from the side of the fairway, where he was waiting to cross the creek to the green.

"You got it!" Dylan smiled as he put his wedge in his bag.

"Nice shot," Hope told him. "You hit that one too well!"

"Thanks," Dylan smiled. "Sometimes I'd rather hit a really good shot and be further away."

"Right?" Hope agreed. "That moment of connection … that's it! That's what's transcendent, not making birdies. That's what we really play for."

"You're the pastor," Dylan joked. "I'll defer to you on transcendence and the meaning of golf." He picked up his bag and they headed towards the bridge. "Anyway, to answer your question, almost all of my close relatives are dead. My mom does have a younger sister, Glenda. She was committed to a psychiatric institution before I was born. I've never met her. Mom doesn't like to talk about her. She never married, never had any children, at least as far as I know."

"How awful!"

"I don't think Judge Smails and Grandma Pookie were very loving parents," Dylan told her. "Their oldest child, my mom's brother Gavin, killed himself when he was just about my age."

"Oh my gosh," Hope sighed. "How horrible! Your poor mother! How hard all that must have been for her."

"It was," Dylan agreed. "Mom moved to Missouri right after he passed. Judge Smails bought some rental properties there for her to manage. They've added more since. After Gavin died, even when I was young, he acted more like her boss than her dad. But, he did make sure I learned how to play golf. He really did love golf. Got to give him some credit for that, I guess!"

"His only grandson! I guess he would …"

"No," Dylan interrupted. "Gavin had a son, before he died. Spaulding was his name. He's dead too—drowned. Nine or ten years ago, I think it was. I only met him once, maybe twice." He stopped to let Hope cross the bridge.

"I played golf with Spaulding and Judge Smails once," Dylan continued on the other side. "It might have been the last time I visited North Platte, before I came out to Mom. At Bushwood, their country club on the lake. Spaulding was horrible." He shook his head. "It was sad. The Judge really came down on him! I wasn't very good, but I was a lot better than Spaulding. The Judge really let him hear about it." Dylan kicked the turf with his toe. "Like I said, he was a miserable old bastard. Seriously, who judges their grandsons by how good they are at golf?"

Hope looked over at Gabriel as they walked up to the green. His ball was sitting far enough out of the trees to be playable. He'd left his bag and walked all the way up past the hole to examine his chip shot. She could tell from the look on his face how determined he was to make it. He looked like Bison. Hope shuddered a little at the thought of Big Poppa getting invested in Gabriel's golf game.

"OK Champ," Dylan encouraged him from the side of the green. "Drop the mike on it!"

Gabriel looked at her. "Knock it in the hole and strut off the stage like a rock star," she translated. He smiled, nodded his head, and re-examined his line one last time.

He hit a nice little chip shot. "Good one!" Hope told him as it rolled out just slightly right and a few feet past the hole.

"Good effort!" Dylan agreed, already lining up his long putt from the back of the green.

"NOOO!" Gabriel shouted. Hope saw heads turn in the parking lot. She stayed quiet, fearing the worst. Dylan never looked up from his putting stance. He hit a solid putt that rolled past Gabriel's ball and settled about the same distance past the hole.

Taking her cue from Dylan, Hope grabbed her six iron and quickly stepped up to her chip shot without waiting for him to mark. She played a simple bump and run that came up just short. "Very nice!" Dylan said. He gave her a short golf clap. "That's a solid par!" He knocked her ball back to her and looked over at Gabriel. He was still holding his wedge over his head, watching them. "What do you say Champ," Dylan called. "Good good?"

Gabriel looked at Hope again. "He means do you want to agree both your putts are good? Like TW and Jaybird did on that hole where you made the long putt from the front of the green."

He kept looking at her. "Does that mean we get ice cream?"

"Yep," Dylan nodded. "If your mom says it's OK we do—I lost the bet that I'd make it from back there."

They both looked at Hope. "OK," she smiled. "Let's go see if they have ice cream!"

The early season ice cream selection at River's Edge was not spectacular. Fortunately Gabriel found something called a 'Choco Taco' that he couldn't live without. Hope and Dylan settled for frozen Drumsticks and they sat down on the patio next to the putting green.

Gabriel devoured his ice cream taco before Hope could unwrap her cone. "Do you want to putt while we enjoy our ice cream like civilized people?" she asked him with a smile. He blushed and rolled his eyes, but grabbed his putter and a couple of golf balls. "So, have you found out anything interesting about your grandfather's estate?" Hope asked Dylan as they watched Gabriel putt. "Any Rembrandts? Golf bags full of unmarked bills?"

"No, not yet," Dylan laughed. "But I've seen enough to understand why Gwen wanted me out here."

"Like what?" Hope asked. "If you can say …

wouldn't want you to give away any family secrets!"

"No," Dylan shook his head. "Who knows, maybe Judge Smails left something to your father. His lawyer, Cottleston, has the will. Like I said, he's just getting back in town tonight."

"Then what seems fishy?"

"How rich he was!" Dylan looked at her. "He didn't just own property in Missouri. There's a bakery in Omaha. There's a chain of lumberyards in Minnesota. There are restaurants in Dallas and Houston. And for all I know, that's just the tip of the iceberg!"

"But his family was rich, right, before him? Maybe he inherited it? We heard that his dad—my grandfather, the Senator—was a real big deal. Wouldn't that have all gone to your grandfather?"

Dylan nodded. "Right, absolutely. The Senator was a big deal, that's for sure! The Charles Foster Kane of North Platte." He rolled up his ice cream wrapper. "And I'm sure none of his money went to your father, where it could have done your family some good. I'm sure it all went to Judge Smails and his brother and sister, before they died." He tapped the wrapper on the table. "But that's not it. Judge Smails had money coming in, not just family money."

"Money from all his different businesses?"

"No, money going out to his businesses! I found a bank statement, from a bank in Omaha. Every six months or so, Judge Smails got big cash deposits in an account there. From offshore banks, in the Bahamas and the Cayman Islands.”

“Why would somebody in the Bahamas send money to Omaha for a Judge in North Platte?”

“Exactly!” Dylan nodded. “I’m not sure, but what I think happened is Judge Smails moved that money into his different businesses. Then he sent the so-called ‘profits’ from those businesses back to the people who sent him the money from the Bahamas.”

“So that the money they got back from Judge Smails …”

“Was clean as the whitest snow. Just the humble proceeds of a proud American lumberyard in the heart of Rochester.”

“Just like Jason’s family giving their drug money to our church.”

“Kind of. But on an industrial scale. Millions of dollars! Maybe more, depending on how long it went on.”

“And now? With the Judge dead? What happens to those businesses?”

“Depends on his will,” Dylan told her. “We just won’t know until his lawyer notifies the family about the will. You and your dad might be entitled to notice … or maybe not, in Nebraska. This lawyer Cottleston would probably squabble about it. Doesn’t really matter. The will is going to be a public record soon enough, after Cottleston probates it.”

“Your mom—she could be a millionaire?”

“Possibly,” Dylan acknowledged. “You never know.
Somebody washed all that money through Judge Smails,
made him rich beyond what his dad could have ever
imagined. Most likely, the people who set that up, they
made some sort of provision for Judge Smails’ death.”

Hope shook her head. “That’s amazing!”

“Oh, that’s just the tip of the iceburg!”

“What do you mean?”

“Well, generally when somebody’s involved in a
criminal scheme like this, and they get murdered, the
criminals they’ve been scheming with are the prime
suspects.”

“They would have killed him?”

“Maybe,” Dylan nodded. “But we don’t even know
who ‘they’ are yet. That’s the next step, that and finding
out what his will says.”

“Sounds like you’ve got a lot of work ahead of you!”

Dylan smiled. “It won’t be very fast-paced. I’m
hoping to play a lot of golf. Speaking of which …” They
looked over at Gabriel, who’d wandered across to the
driving range and was enthusiastically whacking
somebody’s leftover balls with his putter.

Hope shook her head. “Gabriel!” He looked back at
her. “Come on, we’ve got to get ready to meet Grandpa
and Uncle Bison!”

"Uncle BISON!" Gabriel yelled, though not so enthusiastically as he'd been doing. He shuffled back towards the patio, waving his putter in the air.

"Maybe later this week," Hope told Dylan, "we can get together again. Maybe even play golf again." She looked at Gabriel holding his putter. "Would you like to play 18 holes the next time we play with Uncle Dylan?" He nodded.

"OK," Dylan smiled, "That's a plan! Even the Judge couldn't argue with that!"

Twelve: Danny
Putting Green
Bushwood Country Club
North Platte, Nebraska

"We've checked every gas station, truck stop, and fast food joint between here and Edgewater. Nothing! If Ivanka drove all night, killed him, got back to her family there by dawn, she did it without leaving a trace." Chief Riggs slapped a ball aimlessly across the putting green. "As far as we can tell, there's nothing's missing, nobody saw anything, and the only fingerprints in that whole house are his, hers, and the damn cleaning lady's."

"What about her?" Dougie asked, sending a ball chasing after the Chief's.

"She was at midnight Mass the night he died," Riggs replied. "Forty people saw her there. Rosa's a devout Catholic, goes to Mass most every day, never had so much as a speeding ticket. She'd been with Smails for more than twenty years. Pookie, rest her soul, made sure Rosa actually got paid decently. I guess she could have snuck over and done him in right before Mass. Or right after. But why? What's in it for her?"

"Not working for Judge Smails any more?" Danny sent his ball after theirs and they started walking slowly down the putting green. They'd been out here for about ten minutes, listening to Chief Riggs recant his struggles with the case.

"Maybe," Riggs shrugged. "The Judge could bring

out the worst in people. But Rosa doesn't strike me—doesn't strike anyone—as the murdering type. And she's a small woman too—about Ivanka's size. It's hard to imagine either of them overpowering the Judge, shoving that shower rod down his throat. Not if he was conscious at least. Not if he fought back."

"Any reason to think he couldn't fight back?" Danny asked. "Did they do an autopsy?" He wasn't quite sure exactly how or why the mystery of Judge Smails' murder became so captivating. But getting ready to leave Augusta, after the Judge's two New York law school buddies practically bum-rushed them out Magnolia Lane, Danny had suddenly decided to see it through with Dougie. He'd been a little uneasy about inviting himself to North Platte, but Dougie welcomed the idea. Said he'd appreciate Danny's support and that it would be good for them to work together.

They got to North Platte late last night. It was the first time Danny had been back since Dad's funeral. The first time he'd been to Dougie and Heidi's since their youngest daughter left for college. It felt strange. Their house was so silent without any kids. It felt even stranger seeing some of Mom and Dad's old furniture again.

"Autopsy?" Chief Riggs chuckled. "That shower rod was sticking out his throat when they hauled him away. Cause of death was pretty well established. So, no, they wouldn't have tested him for drugs, or poison, or anything like that."

Dougie tapped his ball into a hole. "So really," he paused. "It sounds like nothing's changed since last weekend. Since before we went to Augusta. You told me then it was somebody who knew him. That or it was some kind of professional hit man."

The Chief laughed. "Professional hit man! Did I say that?" He missed his putt. "Well, I guess that's possible." Riggs stood up straight and scratched his head. "Funny I would have told you that. Last weekend, when we talked, you'd have told me there was that kind of money in killing Judge Smails, I'd have laughed. I mean, sure, he inherited that house from the Senator, probably a decent chunk of cash, but Judges don't get paid that much, you know? I never figured the Judge to have the kind of money somebody might kill for." Chief Riggs waved his putter back and forth.

"Makes sense," Dougie nodded. "The Judge never threw any money around, that's for sure." Riggs chuckled. Dougie looked at Danny. "But Chief, sounds like now you're thinking maybe that's not so crazy? Maybe somebody might've killed him for his money?"

"Maybe enough money somebody might've hired a pro to kill him?" Danny added.

"I don't know," Riggs shook his head. "I just don't know about that. But his grandson's here now. He's asking a lot of questions. About Judge Smails' money.

He's asked a lot of people, they talk—you know how people are!" Riggs looked at Dougie, who looked shocked. "Apparently there's a lot more money than anyone ever knew about."

"Grandson? What grandson?" Dougie shook his head back at Riggs. "Spaulding died … gosh," Dougie stopped and thought. "Before Pookie passed. Several years before, I'm not sure …."

"Not Spaulding," Riggs interrupted. "Kid named Dylan." The Chief nodded at Dougie. "Son of the Judge's middle child, Gwen, not sure you'd remember her? She moved away, to Missouri it turns out, right around the time Spaulding's dad Gavin killed himself. Probably not many folks here remember her. I didn't really remember her. Totally forget about her for years, right up until this Dylan kid turned up last week, to be honest with you."

"Just how many kids did Judge Smails have?" Danny interjected.

"Three," Dougie replied slowly. "He had three kids. Gavin was his oldest. He's the one everyone remembers. Quarterback of the football team, smart as a whip, could do no wrong. Went off to Princeton, then law school at Stanford." Dougie paused. "Made the Judge so proud, he hardly ever stopped bragging on him."

"What happened?" Danny asked.

"He shot himself in the head," Dougie said. "Judge Smails took it hard. Didn't play golf for a week. Went out to California, dragged Spaulding back here. He was just a kid, maybe seven or eight? The Judge said his mom was a tramp and a drug addict, blamed her for Gavin. The Judge and Pookie took custody of Spaulding, kept him here. They had some big legal fight over it. Of course the Judge won. He might even have had her committed, something like that. Anyway, Pookie tried her best, but Spaulding ended up getting into drugs himself." Dougie shook his head and smacked his ball clear to the other end of the putting green, back up towards the pro shop. "Died right here at Bushwood, Spaulding did. Passed out in the pool and drowned."

"Yep," Chief Riggs agreed. "High on dope. Drowned with a big old grin on his face. Judge Smails wouldn't let us investigate though, to find out where he got the drugs. Said it would look back for Bushwood. Made us write it up as an accidental drowning." Chief Riggs and Danny smacked their balls up after Dougie's.

"The Judge's youngest," Dougie continued as they walked back up across the green. "She was another heartbreaking story. Glenda, that was her name. She was born with horrible birth defects, needed full-time care her whole life. Haven't thought about her in years, no idea if she's still alive or not." He shook his head. "That poor woman!"

"Really?" Chief Riggs asked. "I don't remember that! I remember Gwen, a little bit, but not a younger daughter.

How horrible!" He shook his head again. "Pookie and the Judge really had bad luck with their kids, huh?"

"The Judge never talked about them," Dougie replied. "Not after Gavin died." Dougie rapped his ball back down towards the middle of the green. "When Gavin died, it really hit the Judge hard. He was never the same man after that. Never talked about any of his kids again. Not once that I remember. I totally forgot Gwen, their middle child. She was really quiet … I don't really remember her at all either. The Judge never said anything about her having a baby, nothing about another grandson."

Danny slapped his ball down past Dougie's. "But now this Gwen and her Dylan grandson: they're all that's left of the Smails family? Does that mean they'll get everything?"

"All that's left of the immediate family," Chief Riggs corrected him. "You start adding up cousins, nephews … the Smails family have been a big deal here for a hundred years. More! Since statehood, I imagine. Won't know for sure who gets what until tomorrow night though. Sterno Cottleston's gonna read the Judge's will."

"They're already setting up for it," Dougie added as Chief Riggs played back to the middle of the putting green with them. "In the small dining room."

Danny tried to imagine any circumstance where he'd think leaving instructions for his will to be read over cocktails and appetizers at his club sounded like a good idea. "And anyone can just show up for that?"

"That's what Stewie said," Dougie nodded. "Said those were the Judge's instructions. Open to all." He shook his head and smiled. "Didn't make any sense at first."

"Still doesn't!" Riggs blurted out. "Never heard of nothing like it. Never had any will reading in North Platte, not that I know of."

Danny looked at Dougie's knowing smile. "What do you mean, at first?" he asked. "Why would Judge Smails do that?"

Dougie looked at Chief Riggs. "At Augusta," he started, "on our trip, listening to Kellerman and Postlewaite, the Judge's old law school buddies. It was pretty clear they had some serious financial dealings with Judge Smails." He looked at Danny. "Obvious the Judge had more than golf going on with them, wouldn't you say?"

"Chief," Danny shrugged, "you might find this hard to believe, but that Smiley Postlewaite, you never saw anyone so eager to finish his round and get off the course as he was there at Augusta."

"At Augusta?" Chief Riggs shook his head. "Hard to believe."

"But it all matches up with what you're saying," Dougie interjected. "About this Dylan grandson who's asking people about the Judge's money."

"It all adds up to the Judge having more money than

anyone ever knew about," Danny said.

"Which is why he wanted Stewie Cottleston to read his will. Out loud. In the small dining room. Open to all. With cocktails and appetizers," Dougie continued.

"So everyone would finally know how much money he had!" Chief Riggs exclaimed. He hit his ball carelessly back towards the top of the putting green and it rolled neatly into a hole.

"You got to admit, that sounds like the Judge!" Dougie chuckled. "Nice putt!"

"But why would anyone actually show up for that?" Danny asked. "Why does anyone care?"

"Oh, they'll show up all right," Chief Riggs nodded. Danny rolled a putt up next to the hole Riggs' ball was in. "They'll be afraid of missing out on something, curious about the Judge. Oh, they'll all be there. You can bet on that!"

Dougie took a moment and settled in over his ball. Danny felt him focus, relax, visualize, and execute a smooth stroke that sent his ball just past the hole. "OK," Dougie said, standing up. "So we'll go listen to Stewie. 'Cue Bono,' isn't that what they say on TV? 'Follow the money?'" Dougie looked at Chief Riggs.

"I guess it depends on where the money goes," Riggs replied. He looked quickly at his watch and handed Dougie his putter. "Do you mind? I got to get back downtown … already late."

"No problem," Dougie assured him. He took the Chief's putter. "I don't mean to upset you Chief. We don't want to get in your way on this …."

"No, Dougie, not at all!" The Chief reached out and touched his shoulder. "I appreciate having you to talk with, knowing you don't talk about it to nobody—unlike most everyone else in this town! You want to come tomorrow, listen to Sterno drone on, speculate about who might have done the Judge in for how much, I'll be glad you're there! We can lift a drink for the Judge."

"A belt of the finest watered down?" Dougie asked, smiling at his friend.

"He wouldn't have had it any other way!" Riggs smiled back. "Thanks Pro. I'll see you tomorrow night." Chief Riggs nodded to Danny and walked quickly up past the pro shop towards the parking lot.

"The watered down?" Danny asked.

"The Chief was on the club's board once," Dougie explained. "Smails was having the staff water down all the scotch except his brand. Told us it made all his drinks taste twice as good. We've joked about it ever since. Riggs is a good guy."

Danny shook his head. "I'm less and less surprised somebody killed Smails and more and more surprised it took so long."

"Yeah," Dougie muttered, flipping his putter and the Chief's putter back and forth in his hands. "I know you never liked him. But what I told Riggs was true. He really did change after Gavin shot himself. Before that, he had a good side. Sure, he could be a jerk. But he could also be generous. Caring even. After Gavin died, he just turned into a full time prick. Totally lost his bright side.”

“I never ever thought about him,” Danny said. “Not once since I left. North Platte never came up much.” He paused. “I guess I never wanted to think about it much. But I never would have thought he’d have had things so horrible like that, with his kids. Not in a million years.”

“You never know about people,” Dougie said. He fumbled with the putters some more. “Look at you—disappeared one day, Dad and me panicking, thinking you were dead, then you turn up with a pile of money on your lap, wind up maybe even richer than Judge Smails!”

Danny looked down. “I’m not proud of that,” he confessed. “I walked out on Dad. Walked out on you. At the worst possible time! Dougie, I’m so sorry!” He looked up at his big brother. It was a conversation he’d imagined so many times. It felt surreal to suddenly be in the middle of it.

Dougie looked at him in surprise. “You’re sorry?!” He shook his head. “Danny, you were just a kid!! I’m sorry! I was so wrapped up with Dad … I wasn’t there for you!” Dougie chuckled. “Just because you came out OK, that doesn’t make it okay that we weren’t there for you. I’m so sorry you never got off to New Haven like you should have!"

"Thanks Dougie," Danny reached out and touched his brother on the shoulder. "You were always there for Dad. I wasn't. You've got nothing to apologize for, as far as I'm concerned. Neither did Dad." He dropped his arm. The words came slowly. "Dad and I, we never really had this conversation. I'm glad you and I are."

Dougie dropped the putters and wrapped his arms around Danny. "Dad would be so happy," he muttered, "if he could see this. Thanks for coming. Thanks for being here."

"Thanks for having me." Danny hugged him back and they held each other silently for a moment.

When they finally let go of each other, they were both smiling. Everything felt lighter, even Danny's putter he'd had since he was fourteen. "So," he finally said, "I guess there's not much more to do, until tomorrow. About the Judge."

"Yeah," Dougie smiled. "That's when we'll crack the case!" Danny laughed. Dougie glanced back towards the pro shop. "I should get some work done, start catching up. Is poor Minnie any closer to squaring away your membership?"

When they got to Bushwood that morning, Danny went straight to Minnie's office to join the club in hopes of playing with Dougie more than once while he was in North Platte. Maybe it would even motivate him to come back again before anyone else died. "She's still working on it, I think. It's challenging, with the time differences and all."

It turned out joining the CIA would have been quicker and easier than buying a membership at Bushwood. There were character references, background interviews, fitness committees, mandatory member education seminars, and mountains of paperwork at every step. A whole gauntlet of obstacles stood between Danny and the first tee.

Fortunately Minnie—like every one else who worked at Bushwood—loved Dougie. Maybe not enough to break the rules, but enough that she went out of her way to run through all of the unadvertised "non-traditional" membership types with Danny.

One of those, Minnie said, had never actually been used, at least as far as she knew. It was something Judge Smails had set up, of course. If you didn't live in Nebraska, Minnie explained, and you were already a member of two "significant" clubs, on two different continents, you could join Bushwood as an "international multi-affiliated non-resident member" on the spot, for a very low fee. International multi-affiliated non-resident members, she said, could play any time for a nominal fee.

"Judge Smails wanted to invite the Captain of the Links and the Links Officers from St. Andrews to Bushwood," Minnie said. "He wasn't sure what their names were, but he knew that they were all members somewhere else in America already, and of course at St.

Andrews. So he had us set up this membership category, with the two continent rule, so he could make them all members. The Links Officers never came, but the Judge never changed it. I think he was a little embarrassed they never came."

"I guess!" Dougie laughed. "Poor Minnie! I bet she nearly had a heart attack when you showed her your membership cards."

Danny's favorite golf courses were on the northeast coast of Scotland and in the sandbelt southeast of Melbourne. On his first trip to Scotland, he'd arranged a meet up at Royal Dornach with Nigel, an English poker player he'd befriended. To Danny's shock, it turned out Nigel was a member and they were able to play both courses as much as they wanted, whenever they liked. To Danny's greater shock, belonging to that remote links paradise was very affordable. Being a member there had opened doors for him across Scotland over the years.

So when he'd planned his first golf trip to Melbourne a few years later, Danny knew in advance what to look for. He found it in spades at Kingston Heath. For a modest yearly fee, he was guaranteed times there and could play reciprocally not only at the other sandbelt links, but many other fine courses around the world.

"She had no clue," Danny grinned. "It's sad, really. She's run your golf club for what, a hundred years, has no idea where Donald Ross grew up, or what the greatest flat course in the world is?" He shook his head in mock disapproval. "What would Dad say?" It wasn't a joke he'd have felt comfortable telling an hour ago.

Dougie smiled. "You watch out," he cautioned, "she'll stop verifying your outlandish membership claims." He looked back over at the pro shop. "You gonna be OK? I really do need to do some stuff…."

"I thought you were retired?" Danny smiled. "I know," he said as Dougie started to protest, "It's the start of the season. I get it. Can I borrow your truck?" Danny asked. "Maybe I'll go over to River's Edge, see how the other half's living. Might even play nine, if you've got that much time for working through your retirement?"

"Sure," Dougie said, laughing. "That sounds perfect! Heidi will be happy we're home for dinner. I'll get caught up here. You have fun there. We'll worry about Judge Smails again tomorrow." He handed his keys to Danny.

"Thanks," Danny said. He reached out and gave Dougie another long hug. They slapped each other on the back and broke apart. Dougie stood by the putting green fiddling with Chief Riggs' putter as Danny shouldered his bag and started the long trek back to the employee parking lot.

After he dumped his clubs in the back and pulled Dougie's truck out of the lot, Danny decided to take the long way around the lake and across the reservoir. As he drove down Lake Road, past the strip malls and subdivisions, he tried to imagine staying in North Platte his whole life. He couldn't think of anything that could have made him do that. No more than he could think of anything that would have made Dougie leave.

Yet here they were, Danny thought as he turned onto the highway and headed down into town. They'd gotten the difficult topics out and apologized for all the things that weren't anyone's fault. They were working together to solve the murder of a man who, in his own small way, had helped drive them apart.

Really, Danny thought, it was Bushwood that drove them apart, not Judge Smails. He passed the interstate and merged onto the Lincoln Highway. All their silly rules. Dougie not being able to play with both Dad and Danny. That wasn't Dougie's fault either, Danny told himself. He smiled to see the old Highway Diner as he made the familiar turn down the long driveway towards the river and the golf course.

There were stores packed in even closer to River's Edge than Danny remembered. The right side of four and five, the short par 3 and easy par 4 that lined the south edge of the course, had always been out of bounds. Now it looked from here like the buildings had filled in right up to the boundary. He wondered how many times they'd been hit, whether you could bounce a ball off of them and back in bounds.

Danny stopped in front of the creek. He looked back

up the fairway but couldn't see anyone on the ninth tee. Nobody was on the range as he crossed the bridge, but the parking lot was pretty full. Danny grabbed his coat. He made sure Dougie's truck was locked, took his clubs from the back, and strode to the pro shop. He glanced over and didn't see anyone on the ninth green or the tenth tee.

Pulling open the glass doors, Danny saw seven or eight people milling about the first tee, and a couple more standing on the putting green. The shop was empty except for a kid sitting on a stool behind the desk watching Sportcenter.

"How's it going?" Danny asked.

"Huh," the kid stammered, turning away from the TV. "Oh, um, hi." He stood up. "How you doing?"

"Doing good," Danny said. "Looks like you've got a few groups lined up right now?"

"Oh, yeah." The kid leaned forward and tried to peer through the glass doors across the shop. "Two or three groups, I think. Did you have a time?" He pulled a worn clipboard out and set it on the counter.

"No," Danny replied. "It's just me. Just playing nine. I gotta pick my brother up after his work!" He took out his money roll and put a hundred dollar bill on the clipboard. "I checked: there's nobody on nine tee, nobody in the fairway, nobody on nine green, nobody on ten tee. How about you take that," he nodded at the bill, "let me shoot off ten, I'll stay out of everyone's way, no problems for anyone?" He smiled at the kid.

The kid looked up and down. He looked around.
After a moment, he nodded and pocketed the money.
"Thanks!" Danny said. "Have a great evening." He
walked out of the pro shop and grabbed his bag, heading
around the clubhouse to the tenth tee.

As Danny walked past the putting green, he saw a
young woman and what looked like her son standing and
looking at the people on the first tee. "But why can't we
play the other nine holes?" the boy asked her.

"It's another one of their Fuddie Duddie rules," she
replied. "It won't be long! Your putting is really getting
good!" She looked at her watch. "We're not going to see
Poppa and Bison until lunch tomorrow anyway, there's no
hurry." The boy shook his head and stroked his ball into
the hole. He had a good putting stroke.

"Excuse me?" Danny said on a whim. "They said I
could start on ten, if I hurried right over. You two are more
than welcome to join me, if you want?"

Thirteen: Bison
Driving Range
Big Jim's Family Fun Park
North Platte, Nebraska

The mangy green T-Rex standing guard over the putt-putt course kept staring at Bison. He tried to ignore it. He pured another seven iron down the middle of the empty range. The misshapen old Pinnacle might have carried a buck fifty in the crisp Nebraska morning air. He looked up. The T-Rex was still staring at him.

Bison looked back over his shoulder. The two elderly attendants were leisurely rolling out go-carts, laughing at each other. Big Poppa's Land Rover was the only car in the lot. "Don't get many golfers in the mornings," the friendlier one had remarked when Bison asked for a large bucket.

"Don't get nobody in the mornings," the shorter, less cheerful, attendant added, hawking a sizable loogie. "Folks mostly got the sense to get things done."

"Don't mind him." He handed Bison his change. Bison thought about asking for a receipt—it was a business expense and he'd just deposited a big chunk of taxable income—but decided $4.00 wasn't worth it. "This way you can see every ball land—yours are the only ones out there!"

That T-Rex saw every ball too, Bison thought. Every shot by everyone who'd ever foregone go-carts, putt-putt, video games, skeeball and the snack shop to venture out back and step up on these threadbare mats. They looked like they'd been out here under the weathered plywood 'cover' through more freezing winters and burning summers than Bison cared to think about.

As best he could remember, Big Jim's just had go-carts and the skeeball arcade when they moved to Phoenix. Bison smiled. He remembered playing skeeball with his friends. Winning stuffed animals and dashing as fast as they could down to the river to race them downstream and watch them disappear forever, madly throwing rocks at each other's stuffies (and sometimes at each other). You couldn't do *that* at any PGA tour driving range!

It was a long way from Houston. It had been a weird drive. Just a few days ago Bison was hitting brand new balls from immaculately groomed turf in front of rapt spectators, surrounded by the best golfers in the world and a flock of camp followers. Now he was out here with T-Rex hitting these old rocks into this dusty field.

He wasn't sure if there'd been anything here before. The go-carts were always over there, on the other side of the parking lot that circled around the arcade and snack shop, he remembered that. They probably added the putt-putt course and driving range around the time of the Tiger Slam, Bison thought, during the last great golf boom. People used to say Arnie should get a cut of every Tour paycheck. These days, Bison figured, TW deserved an even larger share.

He needed some time alone. They were meeting
Hope and Gabriel for lunch at noon. Hitting balls was a
good excuse to leave Hamilton and Big Poppa and get
away from the Best Western for a while. Apparently there
weren't any luxury boutique hotels with their own art
collections in North Platte. Bison slotted another seven
iron and shook his head. It didn't look like there was much
luxury here at all. He'd just won more money over a
weekend than most of these people would see in years. He
was curious to find out what Hope had learned about their
family history, what kind of roots they had here.

Bison switched to his four iron and sent another ball
soaring. He really was on form, he thought. Glancing
behind him, he saw the attendants still staging go-carts,
oblivious to him. Good. That ball made a *noise*, he
thought. Guy doesn't turn around for that, he's not a
golfer. Perfect. Bison came to Big Jim's, instead of going
to a real range, so he could just think for a while without
having to deal with any golfers.

And he wasn't hitting it any worse than he had with
Big Poppa shaking his crazy cane. The magnutstifier.
Whatever he called it. The snake oil. The same thing Big
Poppa had been peddling his whole life, except this time it
came with transistors and a shiny silver metal wrapping.
And it *did something*. It wasn't a complete fraud, like
Trophy Dogs. Maybe that's why Big Poppa was so
passionate about it.

"It's not a goddamn choke ray, and it can't *make* you hit a good shot." That's what Big Poppa had kept insisting. Sad thing is; he wasn't lying. Bless his heart; he didn't even think it was cheating! "It's like lavender oil, or patchouli," Big Poppa protested. That's what he kept saying. "Lavender oil! If you rub lavender oil on your golf bag—hell, all over your trousers—because the smell relaxes you, is that cheating!? If wearing Chanel #7 cologne reminds you of slipping your hands under Debby Dolittle's bra and makes you play better, is *that* cheating!? This is the same thing!"

Bison had played with a couple of guys whose cologne probably should have been illegal, but he hadn't pressed the point. Big Poppa and Hamilton were more than prepared to argue the issue though. They had sheets breaking down every different rule that could possibly apply from the PGA, the PGA tour, the USGA, the R&A, the LPGA, the NCAA, the NJGA, the Asian tour, the European tour, all the way down to some regional municipal golf association in Western Australia. Last Friday night, after they packed up their pizza and headed back to the hotel, they ran him through their dog and pony show.

The only rules in the entire golf universe, Hamilton and Big Poppa assured him again and again, that could possibly forbid their magic stick were the ones governing equipment. And none of those rules, as written, anywhere in the world, banned the cane. They were 100% sure of it. He could see for himself! They were all right there!

"What?!" Bison first asked in shock and disbelief. "What about the rule against giving John Merritt some kind of mental breakdown?" He'd stared at Big Poppa. "You can't seriously tell me *that's not cheating*! Hell, he knew he'd been cheated! He just didn't figure out it was you, or how you did it!"

He'd stood up to call the tournament office and disqualify himself. Maybe just retire, he'd thought. He remembered warning Merritt how even speculating about heebie jeebie curses might haunt him. He could scarcely imagine what would happen to someone who withdrew after his father claimed to wield the magic staff of curses that smote John Merritt.

But Big Poppa had talked him back down. Just like he always did. "Just because Merritt had a bad reaction doesn't mean it's illegal! If I play with a guy who's allergic to lavender oil—that's not *my* fault, is it!?"

"It's a gray area, Bison," Hamilton had interjected, trying to play the good cop. "There's never been anything like this! The rules of golf—every rule, all these rules, around the world—they were all written by fusty old people." He shook their sheets of rules at him. "People who could never understand something like this. There's no way they could ever have thought of it, so they never made it illegal!"

That didn't sound like a rousing endorsement, but Bison kept listening. First Hamilton had "summarized" how the thing worked. Bison could tell he believed every word of it, just like Big Poppa. It had something to do with nanoneural feedback, Hamilton said. Resonant and discordant wavelength frequency mirroring and distorting to extend, sustain, and adjust the bioelectrical manifestations and byproducts of the human emotional experience, or something like that. Bison didn't believe a word of it. Not at first. But something *had* happened with Merritt. He couldn't deny that, and it kept nagging at him. Their magic staff was pretty heavy and it did have a lot of electronics crammed into it.

At first he was sure it didn't matter one whit whether or not the damn cane actually worked. It was still cheating. You couldn't try your best to hit John Merritt in the head by "accidentally" skulling a wedge and then maintain you didn't do anything wrong because you missed him by fifteen inches. It didn't work like that. Trying to cheat was cheating. At first, it had seemed like such a small point. But as he'd heard them out, and reviewed the actual rules, that one small point, whether or not the thing actually worked, kept getting more and more important.

"It's the USGA rules and the R&A rules that matter," Hamilton had explained. "And their equipment rules are more or less the same in every relevant aspect. You can use any kind of equipment you want—they don't want to slow the wheels of commerce!—so long as it doesn't 'artificially eliminate or reduce the need for a skill or judgment.' That's it! As long as it doesn't make the game easier, they're all for it!"

Bison hadn't seen his point. If the thing didn't make the game easier, what was the point? Wasn't making it harder for the other golfers the same as making it easier for him? If not, wasn't it just a spiteful exercise in cruelty? But they'd kept pressing back, telling him that confidence was just an emotional state: that the skill and judgment required stayed the same, no matter how high, or low, a golfer's confidence might be.

Bison didn't buy any of it until Big Poppa finally shut up about lavender oil for a moment. That's when Hamilton went on his rant about Tiger's red shirt. And that's when Bison started drifting loose from his mooring, when he started to think the kid might actually have an argument.

"Under all these rules," Hamilton proclaimed, pounding the stack of papers, "that red Nike shirt Tiger puts on every Sunday morning counts as part of his equipment." He flipped through their sheets. "There are pages of decisions here about compression garments, patterned shirts, girdles, sports bras … it goes on and on. Nobody can say his shirt isn't considered equipment under the rules. It's just too clear cut. Are you with me on that?"

Bison had to nod, and his first small brick of resistance dropped away.

"Good," Hamilton nodded. "OK, so why does Tiger wear that red shirt?"

"I don't think it's the same shirt," Bison had mumbled. He tried to find some way to disagree, to hold his ground. "They give him a lot of shirts, as many as he wants."

"On Sunday!" Hamilton barked. "Why does Tiger use that particular red piece of equipment every Sunday?" He raised his hands. "Now I know, don't tell me, what the"—he made air quotes—"official story is. That his mom, the Buddhist, started him off on it as a youngster, dressing him in red because it was a 'power' color." He made air quotes again and shook his hands around above his head. "She said that right from the start! She said right from the start that his shirt has power!"

"The kind of power the old men who write the rules of golf could never comprehend!" Big Poppa interjected, leaning in between them.

"Never mind them," Hamilton shushed him, dropping his arms. Bison saw him take a couple of breaths and try to relax. "Never mind them and never mind what the hype machine says. Why does he really wear that red shirt? It's not a trick question. He's got two reasons. First, it reminds him that he's about to kick your ass. Second, it reminds you that he's about to kick your ass. That's it! He's not equipping himself with that red shirt for its UV resistance and stylish flair. He's putting that shirt on so you'll both know he's about to kick your ass! So that he'll be *more* confident and you'll be *less* confident!"

Bison reacted without thinking. "And that's legal?"

Hamilton just stopped talking and smiled coldly at him. Of course it was legal. What kind of lunatic would you have to be to stand up and demand that Tiger forfeit every tournament he'd ever won wearing a red shirt on Sunday? But as Hamilton and Big Poppa droned on about reactive galvanic neurotransmitting agencies and biomass to energy frequency ratios, Bison started to realize they might actually have a point. TW's red shirt was equipment that, if it worked right, boosted his confidence and sapped the will of his fellow competitors. Big Poppa's cane was equipment that, if it worked right, boosted Bison's confidence and sapped the will of his fellow competitors. He remembered telling them, "TW's equipment works a lot better than yours."

Because after two rounds it looked like their magic staff needed a lot more magic sauce. He'd played well, but not unreasonably so. Sukert hit a few spectacular shots, but still trailed behind him. They'd made the cut comfortably, but neither was among the leaders. Merritt had imploded on the greens, but struck the ball beautifully. Their magumifier did *something*—Merritt was proof of that—but you'd have been hard-pressed to say just what—or how much it helped—let alone think it was as anywhere near as effective as TW's red shirt.

Nobody would ever ban TW's shirt, because nobody who wrote the rules of golf would ever really believe Tiger Momma's claim that it had real power. Maybe nobody but Merritt would ever believe Big Poppa's cane had any real power of its own either. If not, if it didn't work, then it couldn't make the game easier. In that case, it wasn't illegal. Just like TW's shirt wasn't illegal if it really was just a shirt, with no real power of its own.

"If it's legal," Bison asked them, "why couldn't you tell me about it?"

"It doesn't work as well," Hamilton explained. "Once somebody knows about it, they start thinking about it, wondering whether it's working. Thinking makes it less effective. Thought is the enemy of strong emotion." He pulled out a fresh sheet of paper and drew a line across it. "We can't just make people get confident, or become tentative, at least not yet." He drew a dotted line curving upwards. "All the magnustifier does is amplify the confidence, or the doubt, that people are already feeling." He drew another dotted line curving down.

"Just like TW's red shirt!!" Big Poppa interjected, pointing at Bison.

It hadn't worked very well, if at all, even when Bison didn't know about it. Now, according to Hamilton, it would be even less effective. If it didn't work, it wasn't against the rules. That much was clear. He knew it was still cheating though. The surest sign of that was how much Big Poppa believed in it. It would be out of character for him to get so excited over something that was totally on the up and up. But still, there was cheating and there was breaking the rules. They weren't always the same.

If it wouldn't even work as well as TW's shirt, which was unquestionably legal, Bison wasn't sure it could be illegal, even if it *was* cheating. And just like all of Big Poppa's gizmos, it didn't work very well, especially now that he knew about it.

So it had come down to whether or not he should withdraw after making his first cut on tour in almost five years because Big Poppa's magic cane made John Merritt freak out. The thought of calling the tournament office and explaining that was horrible. Merritt wasn't in the tournament any more. His peculiar mentality, Bison thought, might well have made him uniquely susceptible: he might be the only one the cane would ever affect at all! Merritt had confidence in his swing, which the staff magnified to produce incredible ball-striking, just as much as it amplified Merritt's putting doubts. Maybe Merritt was just that one golfer in a million who was allergic to Big Poppa's lavender oil?

So he justified not saying anything and playing the last two rounds by telling himself that only Merritt had been affected, and only because of his eccentricities. With Merritt gone, the thing was impotent—and therefore legal—for the final 36 holes. Deep down Bison knew it was cheating, but he took the easy path out because deep down he didn't believe in Big Poppa's magic cane any more than he thought TW's red shirt had real powers of its own.

The last two rounds were predictably unremarkable. Big Poppa's assurances that the maguffifier was going to win him the tournament and then beam him into Butler Cabin wearing a green jacket were predictably delusional. But Bison stayed steady, kept playing well, and felt great about his finish, breaking par in all four rounds. Then, just as they walked up to the eighteenth green on Sunday, a squall moved in. The wind and rain drove scores up coming down the stretch. Several players went full reverse overdrive and Bison wound up tied for fourteenth! It was a fantastic result for him. He had enough money to play the rest of the year and hopes of sponsor's exemptions at some of the smaller events later in the season.

Bison put away his four iron and took his wedge out to wind down. He needed to get back to the hotel and clean up before they met Hope. He was swinging great. Standing here thinking about it, Bison realized Houston had worked out perfectly for him: a strong finish and no mention of the magical cane of curses. It was hokum. It hadn't worked, so it wasn't illegal, so there was no story.

But the drive back to Dallas hadn't been any victory march. Houston had been a colossal failure as far as Big Poppa and Hamilton were concerned. They'd been despondent despite Bison's success. Hamilton spent most of the drive to Dallas mumbling to himself. Occasionally he slapped Big Poppa's shoulder and made him write something down in a tiny pocket notebook. As soon as they got to Bison's apartment, Hamilton took the notebook and the cane and glumly shut himself in the guest room to call his father and report their failure.

As always, Big Poppa bounced back quickly. By the time they stopped for gas, he was already turning around every few miles and sticking his head into the back seat to tell Bison how much better the next version would be; how it was only natural for a radical innovation like this to have a few bugs at first; how they'd get it dialed in this summer and Bison would win the Masters next year; and so on.

Bison had just smiled and nodded his head. He tried not to think about whether Big Poppa had ever actually congratulated him for finishing so well. He tried not to be disappointed Big Poppa hadn't come to Houston just to see him. Bison tried to pretend to himself that he'd never imagined a future with Big Poppa playing a regular part in his life.

He'd figured Dallas would be the end of it, that the next morning Big Poppa and Hamilton would take their leave and go off wherever it was they needed to go. But that changed fast. Hamilton got off the phone with his dad and told Big Poppa they needed more money. Money to buy a new machine that would let them reprogram a certain instrument which they could use to recalibrate the macsnuffifier.

"There is no more money!" Big Poppa shook his head. "No way, no how! He's gonna have to figure out a way to do it with what we got. I can't get any more!"

But Hamilton was relentless. After a time, Big Poppa admitted that yes, he could *ask* for more money, "but not over the phone. We'd have to go there: bend the knee, kiss the ring, the full meal deal!"

While they'd bickered, Bison had picked up his phone. It had been his "official" contact number for about three years, ever since his last agent fired him, and he was hoping people had noticed his finish. To his surprise, amidst the congratulations and sales pitches, there was a message from Hope! "…project on his family, so we decided to come here to North Platte over spring break and see what we could find out. It made me miss you! And Poppa! We want to see you! Gabriel plays golf now, so we thought maybe we could meet up with you at one of your tournaments, later this summer, if that would be OK with you? We wouldn't distract you, I promise! OK, anyway, sorry for the long Fuddie Duddie voicemail. We're here at the Park Motel until Friday, and then back to Shelter Cove …."

"So we go," Hamilton told Big Poppa, nodding. "You bend the knee, we get the money. How soon can we be there?"

"It's about twelve hours," Big Poppa told him. "But I'm telling you, there's no more money." He shook his head. "If you want to waste a few more days, nothing to do but get it over with I suppose. We'll leave in the morning."

"I got a message from Hope," Bison interrupted. "She's in North Platte. With her son." He didn't hear much from Hope. She'd fallen in with a rough crowd at college, started taking drugs every day. Wound up marrying her dealer, at least that's what Big Poppa said. Practically disappeared into the California backcountry where his family grew drugs. Then her husband got shot by some rival gang and now she was raising their son out there, an unemployed single mom.

"North Platte!?" Big Poppa recoiled and shook his head. "That's strange." He stood up and looked at Hamilton. "That's where *we're* going! That's where the money came from, even though there ain't no more of it."

Bison and Hamilton had both looked at Big Poppa, then at each other. It was a heck of a coincidence, if that's all it was. "I'm going with you," Bison impulsively told them. He hadn't seen Hope for a long time. After driving all day yesterday, they'd gotten to town too late to see her last night. Now, as Bison put his wedge away and packed his bag, he was really looking forward to seeing her and Gabriel.

The attendants ignored him as he walked back through the empty lot and packed his bag securely against the back seat of the Land Rover. He drove back across the South Platte to the Best Western. After a quick shower and change of clothes, he walked down and knocked on Big Poppa's door.

"Come in," Big Poppa replied in a hushed tone. Bison walked in and saw Big Poppa lying on his bed in the fetal position. Hamilton was sitting by the TV, holding his face in his hands.

"So, no more money?" Bison asked, seeing their defeat.

"No more Judge!" Big Poppa mumbled in a monotone.

"Judge? What does a judge have to do with it?"

"He was my half-brother," Big Poppa said. "Judge Elihu Smails. He's the one, financed the magnustifier." Big Poppa sat up on the bed. "He wanted to break 80 so bad. To measure himself against other golfers and come out on top."

Bison didn't remember Big Poppa having any half-brothers. "Half-brother? And he won't give you any more money?"

"He won't give nobody nothing!" Hamilton interjected. "He's dead! Murdered!"

Bison was shocked a second time. "I'm … sorry" was all he could say. It was a lot all at once, hearing about an unknown relative and his murder at the same time.

"He was a rat bastard," Big Poppa said. "But we

always got along. He never doubted me, knew I had his same blood in me."

Bison shook his head and tried to steady himself. Big Poppa hadn't moved and Hamilton had his head in his hands again. "We've got to get going," he said. "To meet Hope and Gabriel. At Pizza Gulch."

"I can't," Big Poppa told him. "Tell her what happened. Tell her I just need a few hours—maybe say we'll meet her for dinner later?" He looked at Bison. "He wasn't much, the Judge. He'd have sold me down the river without a second thought. But he always believed in me. I just need some time, that's all."

"OK," Bison mumbled, as he uncomfortably left the room and walked back down to the Land Rover. "What about you believing in Hope? In me?" he thought in the parking lot. That's what he should have said.

The sad thing, he thought as he drove back across the river into downtown, was that Hope probably wouldn't be surprised at all by Big Poppa not showing up for lunch. That was just par for his course.

He parked the car and went into Pizza Gulch. Hope didn't see him at first. He stopped in front of the gum machines and watched them for a minute. Gabriel was so much older than Bison had imagined! He was sitting quietly, kicking his feet softly against the bottom of their booth. Hope looked great! But he could tell she'd been through a lot, that she'd had some hard years and they'd taken a toll.

He walked over to their booth with a smile. "UNCLE BISON!" Gabriel blurted, drawing the attention of everyone in the room. He stood up. Hope smiled and stood up, reaching out to him.

"How'd you know it was me?" Bison asked, taking Hope into his arms for a big hug.

"Because you look like a golfer!" Gabriel told him with a serious look.

"You look great!" Hope added, looking up at him. "Congratulations on doing so well in Houston!"

Fourteen: Dougie
Putting Green
Bushwood Country Club
North Platte, Nebraska

Bushwood hosted a lot of social events. Wedding receptions were the worst. Weddings themselves were just mildly annoying. Members would be aggrieved at not being able to park in their accustomed spots, whether at the bar or in the lot. Photographers liked to spontaneously take the wedding party out on the course for pictures, not realizing how many members saw them as vile trespassers and kept right on hitting, whether past them or at them. But those were trivial nuisances compared to the shenanigans that came with an open bar after dark.

Every time they scheduled a reception at night, Dougie just sat home and waited for his phone to ring. Something always went wrong. Employees taking advantage of drunk guests. Drunk guests taking advantage of drunk employees. Broken windows. Golf carts in ponds. Stolen booze. Bad language. Smoking grass. It was always something. And now, standing under the setting sun at the top of the putting green, watching Angie stock the bar in the small dining room where Judge Smails' will would soon be read, Dougie started having those same premonitions.

He hadn't talked to Stewie Cottleston since they got back from Augusta the day before yesterday. The lawyer hadn't said much about the will reading on their trip. He'd made it sound like a mere formality. But after talking to Chief Riggs yesterday and listening to hot takes from members all day today, Dougie was starting to worry it might turn into a reception level disaster.

It was Judge Smails' last chance to be the center of attention—the thing he loved the most—at Bushwood: the place he loved the most. It was the Judge's only chance to flaunt his heretofore hidden wealth. It was his final opportunity to dispense blessings and curses upon family and friends. There was no chance, Dougie thought, it would be just a formality.

Chief Riggs was right about one thing: everyone would be there. They'd already added several extra rows of folding chairs at the back of the small dining room, which actually seated more people than the main dining room, albeit under a lower and less majestic ceiling. People were already showing up, milling around awkwardly like they did before weddings. Or funerals, Dougie thought glumly.

Dougie turned around, unlocked the door, and went back into the empty pro shop, locking the door behind him. He'd left the vacuum cleaner out, just in case somebody starting talking about the Judge and he needed an excuse for ignoring them. He was sick of Judge Smails. He didn't care who thought Ivanka did it, or didn't do it, or who else anyone thought might have done it. He didn't want to know anymore.

Because it had become all too painfully clear to Dougie that Smails wasn't murdered by some criminal he'd sentenced or a burglar he'd cornered. It was somebody he knew, or it was a professional hired by somebody he knew. That's what Chief Riggs told him the day after they found the Judge's body. The only thing that had changed is now they knew about the Judge's money—his own hidden money *and* the money he'd taken from Kellerman, Pork Chop, and the rest of them. That made it even more obvious the killer had some connection to Bushwood, something to do with golf.

Dougie didn't like that. He believed in the integrity of golf as much as he believed in anything besides Heidi. Knowing the killer was part of *his* world, the golf world, made him feel dirty and uncomfortable. He felt let down, no matter who did it. He'd devoted his life to golf. He'd always believed there was something inherently noble about the game. The Judge's murder—and now hunting for his killer at Bushwood—was rapidly diminishing Dougie's faith in everything except Heidi.

He flipped the vacuum on and pushed it back and forth a few times, in case somebody was watching. He'd told Danny to meet him here, so they could walk over together. That was the one good thing that had come from Judge Smails' murder, Dougie thought, this fresh start with him and Danny. All the things they'd avoided talking about all those years came out pouring out yesterday. It started on the putting green, continued through dinner with Heidi, and wrapped up with a glass of scotch on the porch. By breakfast this morning, it was all just bad memories.

Heidi was so happy! She was an only child. In many ways the split between Dougie and Danny had weighed heavier on her than on Dougie. She'd always thought about it more. She'd been the one who'd tried the hardest to stay in touch with Danny, sending Christmas cards every year and cards from his nieces on his birthday. Heidi and Danny were still talking about who killed Judge Smails when Dougie went to bed.

Minnie had finally verified Danny's international multi-affiliated non-resident member status late this afternoon, so he was a member now, even if he didn't know it yet. Dougie had dropped him off at the airport car rental this morning. He'd insisted on renting a car even though Dougie was happy to lend him his truck. At first Danny wanted to just buy a car, but he decided that would take too long. That's when Dougie had started realizing hanging out with his rich brother was going to be different from knowing he had a rich brother. Danny was already making plans for them to visit Dornoch.

There was a knock on the window. Dougie turned to see Chief Riggs peering through the door. He shut the vacuum off and let the Chief in. "Still working on the spring cleaning?" the Chief smiled. He knew perfectly well what Dougie was doing.

"There's a couple of spots …" Dougie tried to grin back. "How you doing? Ready to get this over with?"

"I guess," Chief Riggs shook his head. "Apparently the Judge left Sterno a whole script, wrote the whole thing out, strict instructions! Everything absolutely confidential, of course."

Dougie tried to smile. "Naturally! I bet he's been telling everyone about it all day in the bar at Big Game."

"Yes and no," Riggs allowed. "He's been holding court since about 11:30. But he swears it's all in a sealed envelope! According to Sterno, nobody, not even him, knows exactly what the Judge's will says, what his instructions are."

"Didn't Stewie write the damn thing?"

"Who knows?" Riggs shook his head. "Maybe Judge Smails wrote it, had Sterno sign it blind, some kind of lawyer trick." He smiled. "I know one thing: I'll bet dollars to donuts the Judge's will has one of those provisions where anyone who challenges it gets nothing. Can you imagine the Judge leaving that out?" Riggs smiled. "Nobody's going to mess with the Judge on this, he's gonna get everything his way one last time."

"You been down there with them all day?"

"No," Riggs grinned. "Looks bad! You know that. Checked in a couple of times, that's all. Had to go back and forth to the office, pretend like we're doing more than just waiting to see what happens tonight."

Dougie looked at the Chief. "I feel like it doesn't even matter who did it. It was a golfer! It was somebody who played golf with the man!" He shook his head. "I just can't believe any golfer would do something like that."

"Yeah," the Chief nodded. "It sure would be a lot easier on everyone if it was some career criminal out for revenge, or a burglar, something like that. You bet! Or even if it was Ivanka, obviously that wouldn't have shocked anyone. But there's just no evidence. We got the phone records today: the Judge called Ivanka in Colorado an hour or two before they say he died. Talked for fifteen minutes, they did. So unless you think the Judge chatted with her family for fifteen minutes while she was on her way to kill him, Ivanka's pretty definitely in the clear."

Dougie wasn't surprised, but it still wasn't entirely easy to hear. It just made it even more certain the killer was somebody he knew. Somebody who'd played golf with the Judge. Probably somebody he'd played with. Somehow it made Dougie feel ashamed of himself, like *he* was guilty of something.

There was another knock on the door. Dougie saw Danny's thousand watt smile and felt better. He smiled back and opened the door. "Looks like quite a crowd!" Danny said. "Chief," he nodded. "You think we should head over?"

Dougie looked at Chief Riggs, who'd already started for the door. Dougie looked back over the pro shop, as was his habit. He tried to remember the last time he'd seen the Judge in the shop. Nothing came to mind. All the years blurred together. He shook his head, turned out the lights, and followed them, locking the door and checking it twice.

As soon as they left the pro shop, Dougie realized the crowd in front of the small dining room had grown considerably. He saw a lot of Bushwood members, but there were also plenty of people he didn't recognize.

"Let's go around," he told Riggs and Danny, motioning towards the kitchen entrance. They followed him back past the dumpsters and in through the kitchen, mumbling their apologies to the staff assembling appetizer trays.

"Must be half the club here," Riggs said as they walked into the noisy crowded room. Dougie saw Stewie Cottleston sitting in the front of the room at a small table, scribbling on a yellow pad. There were two or three other tables against the back wall with appetizers. There was a crowd of people surrounding the stand-up bar on the far side of the room. There were ten or fifteen rows of folding chairs—Dougie guessed there must have been 200 chairs!

"Twenty bucks says there aren't this many at his funeral," Dougie muttered to Riggs. On Sunday the Judge would be laid to rest in the Smails family vault at North Platte Cemetery. On Masters Sunday. Dougie was already worried none of the Judge's Bushwood cronies would show up.

"No open bar at funerals," Riggs muttered back. "No bet. But where did they all come from? I see the Judge's cousins, Spencer and Wainwright." He pointed to the middle of the room, where a group dressed in black sat silently. "Must be the rest of the Smails family, sitting there with them."

"Where's Mrs. Smails?" Danny asked? "I don't see any mysterious European beauties?"

"Doubt she'll show up," Riggs answered. "Why would she? Walk into this lions den?"

"They got the phone records," Dougie updated Danny. "It couldn't have been her."

"So you think the killer will be here?" Danny asked excitedly. Dougie looked over at Danny staring at the Chief. Danny really had sunk his teeth into the Judge's murder, Dougie thought. There was no denying that. But it wouldn't be any reflection on Danny, if somebody in this room *had* killed the Judge. It wasn't personal to Danny like it was for Dougie.

"I'd say the odds are better than 50/50," Riggs allowed. "Less of course I was right last weekend and it was some kind of hired gun."

"I don't see Kellerman or Postlewaite," Dougie pointed out. "The Judge's law school buddies. They're suspects, because of all the money."

"Probably they're the ones most likely to have hired a killer," Danny added.

"I guess," the Chief muttered. "Can't imagine anyone hiring any contract killer here in North Platte. Not one that knows what they're doing at least."

"So who else *is* here?" Danny asked. "The Smails family down there in black, they're not from here? What about all the rest of these people?"

"Spencer and Wainwright live in Lincoln," Dougie said. "Judge Smails used to talk about them. They're lawyers, in some big firm there."

"Do you think they're connected to Kellerman and Postlewaite?"

"Doubtful," Dougie replied.

"Wouldn't be like Smails, sharing his good fortunes with his cousins like that," Riggs added.

"Anyway," Dougie added, "a lot of them crowding around the bar are just regular Bushwood members. Like the Chief said: here for the free booze and fear of missing out on something."

"And it's not like there's a lot else going on, Tuesday night," Riggs shrugged.

Dougie looked around the room. He was amazed how many kids there were. "Who brings their kids to a will reading?" He pointed to a group sitting on the appetizer side of the room. It looked like a boy of eight or nine accompanied by his teenage brothers, their parents, and a grandfather.

"That's Gabriel!" Danny interjected. "And that's

Hope, his mom, sitting next to him. I played the back nine at River's Edge with them yesterday. She said something about meeting up with her dad and brother—maybe she meant brothers? That's probably them. She said Gabriel's dad died. Sounded like it was some time ago. He's a neat kid! Great putter!"

Riggs looked at Hope, then at Danny. Dougie looked more closely at Hope. She looked like a supermodel. "I gotta start playing River's Edge more," Riggs muttered to Dougie. The Chief looked back at Hope. "Wait, that's not her brother! The guy next to the kid—Gabriel? That's Smails' grandson! That's Dylan, the lawyer! The one who's been asking all the questions about the Judge's money! What's she doing with him?"

"Maybe you're not the only one she's been playing golf with," Dougie teased Danny.

"Probably not," Danny laughed back. "I didn't really even talk to her much." He shrugged. "Mostly I just hung out with Gabriel. They live in California. A tiny little town called Shelter Cove. They play a community nine-hole course there, wrapped around a runway perched on the edge of the Pacific. It sounds fantastic!"

"So what does her family have to do with Dylan?" Riggs asked.

Dougie looked past Hope at the other three grown-ups. The teenager he'd never seen before. The old man didn't look familiar. But there was something about the other man. He was a big guy! He looked to be 40 or 45 and he was a golfer. A good golfer! Dougie was sure of that. He could see it in the color of his face, the cut of his navy windbreaker, the shine on his leather shoes. But he couldn't quite place him.

One of Dougie's tricks when he couldn't remember somebody's name was to picture their golf swing. He was much better at swings than faces. As soon as he put a club in the man's hands, saw the powerful arms under the navy windbreaker start to waggle, he had it: "That's Bison Tromble!"

Danny gave him a clueless look but Dougie heard Riggs take a sharp breath. "Jesus," the Chief said. "You're right! That's Bison and that's Tommy Tromble right next to him! With that big silver cane."

Dougie looked at Riggs. Danny gave them both another puzzled look. But just then the lights dimmed and dimmed again. "Ladies and Gentlemen," they heard Stewie Cottleston say over the Bushwood PA, "can you please take your seats. Seats please!"

Stewie stood up and motioned with his hands at various groups of people, walking back and forth until the crowd settled down. He walked around and stood in front of the table. "On behalf of the Honorable Elihu Smails," he started, "I'd like to thank you all for coming tonight."

The Bushwooders gave a spirited ovation, toasting him and shouting encouragement. He gave them a quick bow, walked back around the table, and sat down. "My instructions are very specific," he continued, lifting up an envelope. "I was given this sealed envelope by Judge Smails last year, on his birthday. Every year, on his birthday, he'd give me a new sealed envelope and take back the old one. 'Didn't earn your money this year,' that's what he'd always say." Stewie paused. "But his instructions never changed. I was to arrange for this gathering, here in this room, open the envelope, and follow his directions. Nothing more, nothing less."

They dimmed the lights again while Stewie opened the envelope. Dougie thought it looked like there weren't a lot of pages in it. He hoped that was a good sign. Cottleston briefly flipped through the pages and started reading.

"At the end of every remarkable life," he began, "the fruits of one's successes must be distributed to the worthy family and friends one leaves behind. For those of you who aren't just here for the free booze..." Stewie stopped and looked up. "It says we're supposed to announce last call now" he said, looking towards the bar.

"Last call!" Angie immediately responded with gusto. Dougie smiled. They'd suffered through plenty of after-dark incidents together. Thankfully, only a few hardcore drinkers shuffled over to have one last round on the Judge. Angie would get shut down in no time. Maybe this wouldn't turn into a circus reception after all.

"…it is my duty, my honor, and my privilege," Stewie continued, "to share with you the disposition of my worldly estate." He stopped again and looked up. "It says that I'm supposed to explain that what I'm reading is not the Judge's actual will, which will be filed with the court in due course, but rather a summary, prepared by him."

"In that will," Stewie started reading again, "Mr. Stewart Cottleston is named as the personal representative of my estate, in appreciation of all our years in court together. This opportunity to earn an honest fee will undoubtedly mean more to him than any mere gift ever could!"

Stewie paused, as if trying to calculate that fee, and went on. "That will also creates a trust, in the amount of one million dollars, for the benefit of my daughter Glenda, God bless her soul. My beloved home, the Smails family seat, originally constructed in 1866 by the first stationmaster in North Platte, shall pass to my daughter Gwen, on the condition that no child of hers shall ever reside there!"

Dougie, Riggs, and Danny all looked over at Dylan, wondering what he'd done to trigger the Judge's wrath. They saw other people looking at him with the same question. But Dylan had a pretty good poker face, at least as far as Dougie could tell. He just kept watching Stewie, seemingly unfazed.

"My daughter Gwen also gets my six rental properties

on Lake of the Ozarks," Stewie read. "As for the rest of my family: my two cousins, six nephews, and four nieces. Many of you have borrowed money from me, some more than once, and never paid it back. The largest amount in arrears is $25,000. For that reason, I will leave each of you that amount, $25,000, minus the amount of your unpaid debt. I'm sure none of you would want any of the rest of you to profit from your failure and disrespect."

"As you know," Stewie continued, "many of the best times of my life were spent here, at Bushwood. This club occupied a very special place in my heart for a long time. As such, I will be leaving $250,000 to Bushwood. Another $250,000 will be made available on a one-to-one matching basis: my estate will match all other contributions up to that total amount. All those funds will be dedicated to erecting a suitable statue, or other memorial, in commemoration of my life and times at Bushwood, and to ensure that it be appropriately displayed at Bushwood, in perpetuity."

"Next," Stewie turned the last page, "I leave $500,000 to my loving wife Ivanka, on the condition that she never remarry. Some things are too precious … to share." Stewie stumbled a moment and there was an awkward pause. "Finally, in consideration of their many decades of friendship and all the great times we've shared at the National and around the world, the remainder of my estate shall be divided evenly between my dear friends and colleagues Charlie Kellerman and Miles Postlewaite."

Stewie stopped and finished the page. "That's the end," he said. "It says to tell you to all go home now."

Danny looked at Dougie as people started to get up and waves of conversation bounced around the room. "So Kellerman and Postlewaite get a lot?"

Dougie looked at Riggs. "Maybe? I guess?"

Riggs shook his head. "You got me."

"The more the Judge had," Danny went on, "the more Kellerman and Postlewaite get. Everyone else got a fixed amount. They get everything else! The richer the Judge got, the more they'd have coming."

"You think they knew that? You think it was part of their deal with the Judge?" Dougie asked.

"You don't think it would be a little unusual for the Judge to give his old school chums more than his family, his wife, and his beloved country club … combined?" Danny retorted. "Because for all we know, that's what he just did!"

"They did get him on at Augusta," was all Dougie could muster. None of it made any sense. Is that why Kellerman and Postlewaite had insisted on not cancelling their trip? Because they'd sent an assassin to murder the Judge and wanted to hear what the rubes from North Platte thought had happened? Why?

A squabble of voices erupted near the door. Dougie looked up to see Spencer and Wainwright and the rest of the Judge's extended family crowding the doorway, exchanging insults with Bobby and Cliffy McDougal. The McDougal brothers were retired semi-pro hockey players who drank as much as anyone at Bushwood and had never got on well with the Judge. Dougie shook his head and sat back down. They weren't getting out of here anytime soon.

But fairly quickly, things calmed down, people moved on, and the crowd started thinning out. Dougie noticed the Judge's grandson, Dylan, standing in front of Stewie's table, with the Trombles, chatting amicably. It really was Tommy Tromble! Dougie shook his head. He looked so old! Bison was standing there with him. Pork Chop and Chompers were down there too, standing behind Stewie.

Dougie nudged Riggs. "Let's go see what that's all about." They all stood up and walked down to the front of the room.

"… provisions of any *in terrorem* clause could ever preclude a contest on grounds of fraud or criminal conspiracy," they heard Dylan tell Stewie in a confident voice. Dougie saw Stewie starting to heat up, but Dylan stayed calm and in control. "Not that there's any reason we need to get that far out over our skis right now! Like you said, there's still a lot to be done as far as even documenting the nature and extent of the Judge's estate." He looked at Chief Riggs. "And I'm sure the homicide investigation team will need some time to process this information and perhaps reevaluate Kellerman and Postlewaite as suspects given what appears to be not only significant motive but also evidence of possible criminal activity."

"Reevaluate!! You need to go arrest them right now!" Tommy Tromble looked like he was ready to burst a seam!

"You have any reason to think they were involved in the Judge's murder?" Stewie asked him. He stood up and pointed at Tromble. "If not, you shouldn't make reckless accusations."

"The Judge told me!!" Tromble shouted, pointing right back at Cottleston. "When he invested in my business! Told me that's where the money came from. 'Those two New York fat cats I went to law school with,' that's what he said! Said that's where *all* his money came from!"

"But he didn't tell you they were going to kill him," Dylan interjected, raising his hands. "So we need …"

"He did!" Tromble shouted. "He said they'd kill him! If they ever found out who I was, what he was investing in, how much money he'd given me. Elihu said they'd kill us both!"

Dougie saw Stewie's eyes narrow. "How much did he give you?"

Tromble looked at the lawyer, looked at the kid next to him, looked at Bison, and looked back at Dylan, looking like he was trying desperately to find a reason not to answer. But he couldn't. "In all, just about a million," he said quietly.

"What!" Pork Chop let out. "You!? Smails gave all our money to *you*? A million dollars? Oh my God, how could he be that stupid!? Hell! How could I be that stupid!? I swear I would have killed him myself, I'd have known that!"

"You shut your trap McDonald," Tromble snarled back. "You don't know shit. Just stay quiet or I might have to kick your ass again. Did it once, you know!"

"Wait," Stewie held up his hands as Pork Chop started forward. "Let's all just slow down!" He looked at Tromble. "How much of the money is left?"

"It's all been invested," Tromble told him. "We tested a prototype this weekend, down in Houston. Went very well! Then we came back up here, to pick up our next round of investment from the Judge."

"He promised you more?" Pork Chop was even more enraged.

"Not exactly promised," Tromble admitted. "But he'd have given it to me. Absolutely he would have. Based on our results! But they must have found out about it first, like he warned me before."

Dylan raised his hands over his head. "Everybody just take a breath and slow down," he said softly but firmly. He paused and Dougie looked around. It was only their group left in the room, except for Victor and Juan folding chairs. The bar was shut. Angie was nowhere to be seen. It was amazing how quiet it was all of a sudden.

"Thank you," Dylan continued in the same calm tone. "Thank you all." He dropped his arms and spoke even more softly. "Now, nobody's going to solve anything tonight. This is going to be a long, tedious process: following the money trail by painstakingly tracking activity back and forth across accounts. So I suggest we call it a night …"

"We can't wait for that!" Tromble interrupted. "We need more money! For the tool we need to finish the prototype. So we can start making money!"

Stewie scoffed. "There's no way I'm giving any more of the Judge's money to *you*! Even if I wanted to, there's no way I could—as personal representative. It wouldn't be legal."

"Actually," Dylan interrupted, "it might be a tad early to say that. If the Judge did invest in his business—if the Judge's share of that venture is an asset of his estate—then if nothing else you might have a duty to exercise reasonable business judgment with regard to any additional financing requests."

"Reasonable?" Tromble threw his arms up. "It's a no-brainer! We're all gonna get rich!"

"NO!" Everyone fell silent as Chompers' scream echoed around the empty room. "NO!" The dentist's fists were clenched and Dougie could see the nerves bulging in his neck as he pointed at Tromble. "I will never let you!" Trembling, his eyes bulging, he looked at Chief Riggs. "I did it," he yelled. "I killed Smails. To stop them! To save the game!" He looked around the room. "And unless you destroy that damn thing right now, I'm taking every last one of you down with me!"

Fifteen: Danny
First Tee
Bushwood Country Club
North Platte, Nebraska

It was cold. Gabriel looked miserable. Hope stood

behind him with her arms folded, gazing disapprovingly at

them all. Dougie had already retreated to the range, saying

he had lessons scheduled, insisting he wouldn't have any

part in it. But here Danny was, on the tee at Bushwood for

the first time since high school, about to play competitive

golf again. For the first time since he won state. The first

time since Mom got sick.

"18 hole stroke play," Stewie Cottleston was

explaining to the small group on the tee. "Bison Tromble

against Danny Newman. Chompers," the lawyer gestured

at the dentist, "and Tommy Tromble"—he pointed at

Hope's dad—"agree that, if Bison wins…." Cottleston

looked down and read from his pad. "Tommy and the

Tromble family will be free to research, develop, promote,

sell, and/or use the magnustifier as they see fit, without any

interference, criticism, or opposition from Dr. Turin, who

will not mention it or them in connection with any criminal

or civil proceeding." He paused. "They also agree that,"

he looked back at his pad. "If Danny wins, Tommy and the

Tromble family will immediately destroy the magnustifier,

along with any and all related apparatus, equipment, notes,

research, and/or data, and will not take any further action to

research, develop, promote, sell and/or use the

magnustifier, which Dr. Turin will be free to discuss."

Stewie stopped and looked up. "Danny wins, they melt that thing down, and Chompers gets to say he killed the Judge because it was the only way to keep him and his bastard half-brother from ruining golf forever," Pork Chop translated. He spat on the tee. "Bison wins, they get to keep peddling their cane, and Chompers can only talk about our money at his trial." He shot the dentist an angry look. "That about it?"

Chompers nodded. He looked like he was in pretty bad shape. He'd already tried to explain himself to Danny on the range. He'd driven the Judge home from Big Game one night, he said, after Smails had a few too many. The Judge, who'd never beaten Chompers, bragged about his invention, how it would make him unbeatable. The thought of the Judge being able to manipulate golfers' emotions against them like that haunted the dentist for weeks. The Judge never mentioned it again, Chompers said. He figured Smails didn't remember their ride home. He'd gone to the Judge's house that night, knowing Ivanka was out of town for spring break, to plead with the Judge before their trip to Augusta. To beg him not to ruin the game they loved.

"But he wouldn't listen!" Chompers told him. "All he could talk about was finally being able to beat golfers who were better than him! He kept laughing at me, telling me how bad he was going to beat me with it!" One thing led to another. Dr. Turin reached his breaking point. Now the Judge was dead and Chompers was still broken.

Danny still hadn't wrapped his head around the murder itself. Turin seemed so small and inoffensive! He couldn't imagine him shoving a shower rod down Smails' throat, stripping his body in the shower to destroy evidence, and then calmly going home to pack for their trip to Augusta and a few relaxing rounds under the pines.

But he could understand why Chompers found Tromble's cane so disturbing. What fun would it be to have a "friendly game" with somebody who was electronically manipulating your emotions to make you play worse? What if it eventually worked so well it took the challenge out of golf, letting anyone who had their cane dialed in right hit every shot as well as they could? Would it all come down to who had the better technology, whose cane was best able to disrupt the other player's confidence and enhance their own?

Because Danny had quickly realized that, if it did, it could ruin a lot more than just golf. Poker, to start with, would certainly never be the same. But that was just scratching the surface. What about people who worked in meat processing plants and at sewage processing facilities? Would a few strategically placed canes make them love their work so much they'd do it for free? Under unsafe conditions?

"Only thing to do about a cheat is not play him again."

As usual, Dad said it best. And that's what Danny had thought of last night, when Chompers and Stewie entreated him to play Bison. How the first time he'd ever been to Bushwood he'd seen the Judge cheat by sticking his ball marker on the bottom of his putter. How at the time Danny couldn't imagine anyone going to so much effort to cheat. Now, the cane made that seem almost quaint, like a parlor trick.

So last night he'd let Chompers and Stewie talk him into this. Because the Judge was a cheat and he didn't want him to get away with it. Because he agreed the cane was horrible and should be destroyed. But this morning Danny was having second thoughts. Maybe if the cane was a terrible way to cheat, he wondered, the thing to do was not play golf, or cards, or process meat, with unscrupulous people who used canes. Maybe that's what Dad would have said.

"Why can't we play with Danny and Uncle Bison?" Gabriel had his head buried against Hope's side and was looking up at her in confusion. He'd only ever played golf for fun, Danny realized. He'd never seen a serious competition before.

"We'll play with them another time," Hope answered. "They decided to play Fuddie Duddie golf by themselves today instead." She shot Danny a look and then stared coldly at her brother and father, who were standing on the other side of the tee talking to what looked like Bison's caddie.

"Hey Gabriel!" Danny said without thinking. "You want to caddie for me?"

Gabriel looked at him and looked back up at Hope. "What's a caddie?"

"Kind of like an assistant," Hope explained. "Caddies carry bags, rake bunkers, read greens, help their player around the course." She looked at Danny. "Usually caddies get a share of the prize money."

Danny smiled for the first time all morning. "There isn't any prize money, at least not yet." He looked at Gabriel. "But I'll pay you $500 if you want to caddie and I'll give you half of any money I do win!"

Gabriel's mouth opened wide. He looked up at Hope again. "It's up to you," she told him. "But get your money in advance!" She looked at Danny. Her face wasn't quite as cold.

"OK," Gabriel nodded. "I'll be your caddie!"

"Great!" Danny smiled again. He opened his bag pouch, took $500 from his money roll, and handed it to Gabriel. "You carry my bag, follow me. Watch Bison's caddie. They just played in a pro tournament, he'll know what to do!"

Gabriel nodded and took hold of Danny's bag strap, looking nervous but excited. "He'll be fine," Danny assured Hope. "If you want to go do something else …."

"No," Hope interrupted. "I can't wait to see what

other tricks you have up your sleeve!" They exchanged a brief smile and Danny felt his day start to get better.

"Well? Let's get on with this! While we're young!" Tommy Tromble strode confidently to the back of the tee and shook his finger at Stewie. "Newman chickened out. I guess that leaves you in charge. So how about it? Let's get them started already!"

"OK," Cottleston nodded. He reached both hands into his pockets and held his fists out to Bison, who pointed to the lawyer's left hand. Stewie opened it to reveal a single coin. "Bison has the honor." He opened his other hand to reveal a coin and a pebble. "Danny hits second." He paused for a moment and gave them a half-hearted "good luck!"

Danny stepped over to Bison and extended his hand. "Not sure we were ever formally introduced."

"Bison Tromble," he replied in a low monotone, wrapping his giant mitt around Danny's hand. "This is my caddie Hamilton." Hamilton nodded.

"Danny Newman," Danny replied, extracting his hand. "I think you know my caddie, Gabriel." He looked over at Gabriel, who was smiling bashfully. "Gabriel, come shake hands with Bison and his caddie Hamilton." Danny shook Hamilton's hand and watched Gabriel shake their hands.

Bison didn't say anything to Gabriel, Danny noticed. The big man didn't seem very happy to be there. Probably figured it was a waste of his time, Danny thought, playing against some never-was old amateur he'd never heard of.

And after watching Bison take a powerful windup and golf his ball long and straight down the middle of the first fairway, Danny realized he might well be right. Bison had wonderful balance for his size and his larger frame let him generate far more clubhead speed than Danny could ever muster. "Beautiful shot," he said.

But Danny learned long ago never to play anyone's game but his own. Sometimes hitting the green first was more of an advantage than driving the ball further. Making putts was always the most important thing. Everything balanced out over the first five holes. Bison was able to easily reach the par 5 in two, but Danny hit a beautiful wedge shot and matched his birdie. Bison had no more than a seven iron on the par 3, where Danny's five iron found the sand short of the green, but they both made par after Danny's bunker shot hit the center of the flagstick and dropped softly next to the hole.

The sixth was a relatively short par 4. Danny saw Bison put his hand on his driver for a moment, but he quickly pulled out a mid-iron and played a conservative shot down the middle of the fairway instead. He was starting to take this pretty seriously. Bison still hadn't said a word to Danny since the first tee, but now he had his game face on. Danny could see him starting to think more about his shots.

But Bison had never played Bushwood before, and Danny used to know a trick here. If you played down the sixth fairway, like Bison, your second shot had to come in over two bunkers just short of the green. If the pin was cut close to those bunkers, it was hard to get it close, even with a sand wedge. But there was another way, or at least there had been thirty-odd years ago.

"How about the driver?" Danny asked Gabriel. Gabriel nodded and handed him the club. Danny saw Bison turn ever-so-slightly and shoot him a quick look. If you'd never played the course before, it didn't make any sense. But Dougie showed him another shot from here once, before the state tournament. If you hit a really solid driver way left, out over the cottonwoods into the fourteenth fairway, it made the hole slightly longer but offered a much friendlier angle to the green, especially to the challenging front pin positions.

The shot, Danny remembered, was a high fade. He tried to peer through the trees to make sure the fourteenth hadn't been rebuilt or rerouted, but he couldn't see much. He took a quick look at the gallery, but couldn't tell if any of them knew what he was considering. He thought about bouncing his drive on seven at Augusta up towards the second green and visualized the fourteenth fairway as best he remembered it. He teed his ball a little higher, waited until he saw it bounding down the middle of the ridge on fourteen, and let his swing send it out over the trees, right on target.

"You hit it in the trees!" Gabriel exclaimed.

"*Over* the trees partner," Danny smiled, handing Gabriel his driver. "You'll see." Gabriel looked up at him with wonder in his eyes and Danny's smile grew even wider. He glanced over at Hope. She was smiling too.

"Is that the local play?" Bison asked as they started around the lake.

"Hope so," Danny admitted. "I haven't played here in thirty-some years. But I'm betting it's still not the kind of place where things change very fast."

"No," Bison agreed, "I'm guessing that's a safe bet!" He managed a little smile at that, and Danny felt like he'd earned a bit of the pro's respect as they walked around the lake up to the fairway.

As Danny led Gabriel through the row of cottonwoods that separated six from fourteen, he was glad to see that the pin was indeed in front, and that the fourteenth fairway was still there. His ball was in the middle of the fairway at the bottom of the ridge, in the perfect spot. "How did you know it would go there?" Gabriel asked.

"That's where I wanted it to go," Danny shrugged. "Sometimes it works!" He smiled at Gabriel, who gave him another admiring look. "Watch what Hamilton does here, after Bison hits."

Bison played a solid shot that, as Danny anticipated, rolled out 25 or 30 feet past the hole. They watched as

Hamilton took Bison's putter from the bag, walked forward and picked up Bison's divot, and walked back to replace it, neatly exchanging the putter for Bison's iron as they passed. "See how they're working together," Danny told Gabriel. "Going at the same rhythm?"

Gabriel nodded, watching Hamilton replace the divot, pick up their bag, and hustle to catch up. "How long has Hamilton been Uncle Bison's caddie?"

"I don't know," Danny said. "Good question! You should ask them about it, after we're done." They walked across the fourteenth fairway to his ball. The shot was just as he remembered. He settled in over a pitching wedge and, buoyed by his memories, put one of his best swings of the day on it. It flew just past the pin and settled obediently no more than six feet away.

"That's well-played all around," Danny heard Bison call out. He looked up and saw the big man with his putter tucked under his right arm, giving him a polite round of golf claps. Danny raised his wedge in acknowledgment. He glanced over at the gallery in time to see Chompers muster a faint smile.

Danny felt his legs go soft. He dropped his arm just as Gabriel held out his putter. He managed to exchange it for his wedge without falling over, stifling a gasp. Making a murderer smile wasn't something Danny had anticipated. It didn't feel very good. Just because Smails was a jerk and a cheat, and his cane was foul and corrupt, that didn't make killing him right.

He managed to keep moving towards the green, where Bison and Hamilton were already looking over Bison's long birdie putt. "Nice shot," Bison told him, smiling. He was fully engaged now, Danny saw, just as he was having more second thoughts about this whole thing.

Bison looked over his putt for a couple of minutes. He put a great stroke on it but came up about three inches short. "Nice par," Danny nodded, as he walked around his short birdie putt. Somehow, he managed to stay in the moment and not think about anything else but the putt long enough for it to fall in the high side. He wasn't sure for a moment whether that was good or bad.

Danny tried to shake off his thoughts. He picked his ball out and gave Gabriel a half-hearted fist bump. He looked back at the gallery as quickly as he could, trying not to see the murderer standing there among them.

"Nice birdie," Bison told him as they made the short walk to the par 3 seventh. "You really hit that wedge solid!"

"Thanks," Danny nodded. "Yeah, that felt good!" He hesitated for a second. "I meant to tell you: congratulations on doing so well in Houston! Hope said you've been on and off the tour for the last few years, she was really happy for you."

"Yeah," Bison nodded. "Thanks. It did feel good. I was lucky: squall moved in Sunday right as we got to eighteen green, guys blew up behind me.”

“Hey, you didn’t make the tee times, right?” Danny joked. “Gabriel and I were watching you and Hamilton in the fairway—you have great rhythm together! How long has he been on your bag?”

Bison laughed but Hamilton gave Danny a stern look. “I’m not a caddie,” he said in no uncertain terms. “My father invented the magnustifier! I’m here to protect his interests, babysitting Bison and his kooky father.”

Danny saw Bison was a little taken aback by that, but the big man didn’t say anything. “Before today you’ve never carried his bag?” Danny asked, trying to keep them talking. “That’s amazing! It looks like you’ve worked together for years.” He saw Gabriel look at Bison curiously.

“He caddied last week,” Bison said. “In Houston. One round qualifier, two practice rounds, and the four tournament rounds. So I guess this is our eighth time out.” He looked at Hamilton. “He did pick it up pretty quick.”

Hamilton snorted. “It’s not hard! Carry the bag, do the math, help the player’s confidence.” He laughed. “Wait! This isn’t medieval Scotland! We have machines for all that!” He looked at Danny. “At least we will, once Doc Holliday over there is safely locked up and we’re free to finish fine-tuning the magnustifier!”

Danny saw Bison roll his eyes. It looked like the big man wasn’t entirely on board with Hamilton’s plan.

"That's why you didn't win," he asked Bison. "In Houston? Because the cane wasn't magnustifying right?"

"That's right," Hamilton said. "This was just the first trial …."

"I don't know," Bison interrupted. "I don't know what it did." He shook his head. "But it did *something*. To John Merritt. You ever heard of him?" Danny shook his head. "He's a journeyman, like me. Off and on tour for years." Bison paused. "He's pretty tightly wound, Merritt is. Anyway, we played together the first two rounds. *Something* threw him way off kilter, made him feel strange. He made a stink about it. From what they say, it could have been their do-hickey. Other than Merritt," Bison shook his head, "I'm not sure it did anything at all."

Hamilton laughed. "How can you say that? How do you think you got through that Monday qualifier?" He looked at Bison scornfully. "You wouldn't have been in the field, made the cut, or finished where you did without it!" The young man looked at Danny and back at Bison. "That lawyer, Cottleston, made us promise we wouldn't use it today, and now you can't even beat him!"

Danny watched Bison carefully as he processed Hamilton's outburst. The big man dropped his eyes momentarily, but didn't say anything. Danny looked out across the lake and saw that the pin was set hard against the water on the back left part of the green. The seventh might have been the hardest hole at Bushwood. It was almost 200 yards of carry to a narrow green with deep bunkers close behind it. Danny quickly grabbed a six iron, teed his ball, and played an easy draw way short and right, forty or fifty yards from the hole, but safely on dry land.

Bison stepped up on the tee and surveyed the green. Hamilton held out a club and told him "195 to cover, 206 hole."

Bison looked at him. "Are you sure?"

Hamilton shrugged. "That's what it says. It's not like Houston: I wasn't out here early measuring."

Bison looked at him again. He took the club and teed up his ball. Watching the big man rehearse his powerful swing, Danny tried to remember if he'd ever seen anyone get up and down from the center bunker to a back left pin. Because a second later, just as Danny knew he would, Bison played a beautiful shot that was just a little safe, right of the pin. But Hamilton had played a little safe too, with his yardage. Unless they'd moved something, Danny knew 206 was in the bunker, and that's exactly where Bison's ball went.

Danny nudged Gabriel's shoulder and got them heading out around the lake ahead of the pack without waiting to see Bison's reaction. He didn't have an easy second shot, but Bison had one of the most difficult on the course. It was a match play situation now. By moving out in front of everyone, Danny was able to stay in control, getting to his ball and set to play before Bison could get around him to survey his fate. Danny played a very conservative six iron bump and run that trundled safely along the green and settled about eight feet short and left of the cup.

Danny took his putter from Gabriel and walked quickly up to mark his ball. Suddenly he thought of Smails, sticking his ball marker to the bottom of his putter all those years ago. This would have been a good hole for it. He looked back past the bunkers at Sterno and the rest of the gallery, walking around behind the green. He looked back up the lake to the tee, the eighth fairway, and the sixteenth green jutting out behind it. Like Ike's Pond, he thought, it was a beautiful place that had seen a lot of sketchy shit.

Danny managed to mark his ball and meet Gabriel on the other side of the hole, moving him well back of the green. Bison's ball was in the bottom of the bunker, which was good, but it had partially embedded in the damp sand, which was horrible. Danny estimated he had about twenty-five feet of dry land to work with if he went straight at the hole; thirty-five if he played to the middle of the green; and forty-five or fifty feet if he aimed at the very front right corner of the green, a hundred feet away from the hole.

Bison was standing in the bunker now, and Danny saw him weighing his bad options. He stepped around and took some rehearsals going at the hole, but quickly decided against that route. He came back up out of the bunker and walked down towards the middle of the green, looking back up towards the hole. Finally, he got back down in the sand and played a wonderful shot that just barely carried onto the green but rolled out quickly and came to rest some sixty feet from the hole.

Danny put his putter under his arm and clapped. "That's the best shot anyone's hit all day, right there! That lie, from there? Beautiful shot Bison!"

"Way to go Uncle BISON!" Gabriel added, screaming his uncle's name and raising both hands. That made Hope laugh, loud enough to hear over the gallery's applause. Bison raised his wedge in acknowledgement and stepped out of the trap, knocking the sand from his shoes.

"Thanks!" He acknowledged, smiling. "That felt good!"

"Felt good?" Danny turned to see Bison's dad take his hat off and slap it against his thigh. "Dang it Son, this is serious!" He put his hat back on. "This is our future on the line!" He looked at Danny and looked back at Bison, shaking his head. "You don't need the magnustifier to beat him! C'mon now! Get in the game!"

Danny watched as Bison silently made his way down the green and looked over his long putt. After walking about halfway back up to the hole and back down, and taking more than a few deep breaths, Bison managed to put a good stroke on it but left it about seven feet short, right next to Danny's marker.

He walked down to the hole as Bison came back up the green. "That's a solid putt from down there," he told Bison. "I'm not sure how their cane could have helped you much with that! Or from the bunker, for that matter. That was spectacular!" Danny shook his head. "I get how you say it had an effect on that other guy, Merritt, because he *felt* it. But if you didn't feel it, like he did, why do they think it had any effect on you?"

Bison stopped and looked straight at him and Danny realized he'd never considered it like that before. "You have to believe," Bison smiled after a moment, shaking his head. "Not many people can sell something they don't believe in."

There wasn't much warmth in Bison's smile, but Danny tried to smile back with just a little more light. Hope hadn't said much about Bison, but she'd talked enough about their family that Danny had some sense of his history with his dad. Danny thought about that as he looked down at his marker and Bison's ball. It was not obvious who was away.

"I'm still away!" Bison laughed.

Danny looked up. "I'm not sure—it's pretty close."

"No," Bison shook his head, "that's how it all started. With Merritt. Never mind." He stopped laughing and looked down at the green. "Do you want someone to measure?"

"I want to apologize!" Danny paused, choosing his

words carefully as Bison gave him a startled look. "I never thought about how, once they came up with this crazy idea … you never had any choice! Your dad—what you just said. He believes! Maybe that's kooky and maybe it's visionary. Who knows! But I never thought about that, about what it meant, last night. He's your dad! You couldn't say no, once I'd agreed to this."

Bison started to protest. "No, I …."

"Maybe you could have," Danny cut him off. "But most people couldn't." He shook his head. "I got caught up thinking about the past, about Judge Smails cheating. I didn't think about the future, your future, everyone's future, like I should have." Danny smiled. "Dougie had it right, as usual, just like Dad always said: only thing to do about a cheater is not play with them." He took his hat off and looked over at the gallery. "So why are we out here playing their game for them?"

Danny watched Bison look over at Hamilton and his father, who were standing by his bag with their arms crossed, mumbling to each other. He saw him glance over at Gabriel, who was holding Danny's bag with great seriousness, and smile. "So what are you saying," Bison asked slowly. "You're going to just quit?"

"I guess I'm asking if you want to just call this whole thing off?"

"How? We're in the middle of the round. As soon as one of us quits, the other one wins."

"I hadn't got quite that far." Danny thought for a second. "What if we cheat?"

"What?" Bison laughed. "What do you mean?"

"If we cheat together, we'll both be disqualified for it, right?"

"I guess."

"So, let's agree that both of these putts are good. We don't even know who's away, we're both agreeing, and we're both cheating."

"So we're both disqualified?"

"Yep."

"At the same time?"

"Has to be." Danny waved his arms at the gallery. "And they have to deal with their problems themselves."

Bison smiled. "Done." He picked his ball up, handed Danny his marker, and extended his hand. "It's been a pleasure cheating with you!"

Sixteen: Hope
Sixth Tee
Shelter Cove Golf Course by The Sea
Shelter Cove, California

"This reminds me so much of Royal Dornoch," Danny
was telling Peter as they looked down across the runway
from the edge of the course, "but a hundred years ago,
before golf was a business. When the course was just
another part of town and a place for regular people."
Veeka was on the other side of the tee giving Dylan a
history of the coastline to the north. Gabriel, who'd hit it
closer than anyone on the fifth and tapped in for birdie, was
making faces at Irwin, who was sitting up in his stroller
laughing. Hope smiled, basking in the divinity of it all.

"Gabriel do you want to hit first? After your birdie?"

Gabriel turned and looked up at Danny and Peter for a
second. He gave Irwin a final warped grimace. "OK."
Danny kept explaining to Peter how Sam Morse had
changed the history of golf in California by building his
high-end resort at Pebble Beach while Gabriel pulled out
his driver, wandered over, and teed up his ball.

Hope looked over at Danny. "You should show
Gabriel how to hit Peter's shot here—the low running cut
across the tarmac!"

"Yeah!" Gabriel exclaimed. "I want to bounce it all
the way down like Uncle Peter!"

"OK," Danny turned around. "I think probably the
first, and definitely the most important thing is: always

check for airplanes!" He spun around in a circle, pointing to the sky, and then held his hand to his ear theatrically. "Don't see any. Don't hear any. You?"

"Nope," Gabriel smiled. Everyone laughed.

"Alright," Danny said, moving closer to Gabriel. "Now the hard part." He knelt down in front of Gabriel and took his driver. "When you hit the ball perfectly straight," he held the club behind the ball, square on target, "its *face* is exactly square to its *path*. Face and path. Those are the two magic words for shaping the ball." He looked up at Gabriel. "Do you know what those words mean?"

Gabriel shook his head. "Great!" Danny said. "Because if you did, I couldn't help you!" Gabriel chuckled. "But I bet you know what a clubface is!" Gabriel pointed to the face of his driver. "Exactly! So that's easy. Path is a little harder." Danny lay the club down with the head pointing towards the tarmac. "Path is the direction of the club at the moment of impact. If the club swings straight down the line of this shaft," he gestured, "the ball will start straight out on that path. If the face is square to the path," he held his hands perpendicular above the driver, "the ball will start there and go dead straight. If the face is turned," he twisted one hand back and forth, "the ball will start down the path, and turn in the direction of the face. So, one easy way to curve the ball is to swing straight and rotate the face of the club." He took Gabriel's driver and made a couple of swings, showing

Gabriel how his hands rotated to change the orientation of the clubface so that it would face left or right of his path at impact.

Gabriel nodded and Danny handed the driver back. "Take a couple of practice swings," Danny told him. "First, let's see a couple of right turns." Gabriel took a couple of swings. "Excellent! That's it! Now a couple of left turns!" Gabriel rotated his hands and made a couple more swings. "Awesome! OK, now come here." Danny stood Gabriel behind his ball and pointed down the left side of the runway. "See where you want to start the ball— where your *path* is?" Gabriel nodded. Danny pointed back to the fairway. "And where you want the ball to curve— where the *face* is?" Gabriel nodded again.

"OK," Danny said, moving away. "You got this!" Gabriel nodded again and took his stance. Hope saw him fidgeting his hands as he looked down the runway and waggled his driver back and forth. After a moment, he made a good swing and hit the ball well down the middle of the runway. It didn't slice as much as Peter's would, or run as far, but it took three solid bounces and managed to just barely roll out off the right side of the runway into the rough.

"I did it!" Gabriel cheered, doing a little dance with his driver.

"Way to go!" Peter congratulated him, stepping up and slapping Gabriel's hand.

"Nice play!" Danny added, smiling at Gabriel.

"Good shot!" Hope said, watching Gabriel smile back at Danny. It would be terrifying how quickly they'd taken to each other if it weren't so beautiful. Just seeing them together made her smile and feel warm and happy.

"Peter," Veeka said, "we'll all understand if you don't want to bother hitting after that! Great shot Gabriel!" She stuck her tongue out at Peter, who laughed.

Peter took out his sand wedge. "All right, since Gabriel stole my shot, I'm hitting a different one! Gabriel, let's see you bounce it this high!" He dropped his ball on the turf, addressed it quickly, and hit a shot that seemed to go straight up in the air. After a couple of seconds, it just barely landed on the corner of the runway, where it bounced back up high in the air. Everyone cheered.

The rest of them played more conventional drives and they started down the hill. "I can't believe you can play here as much as you want!" Dylan told her. He swept his arm out over the ocean. "This is amazing! And there's nobody out here! My God, back east they'd be lined up for days."

They'd driven down and picked Dylan up at the San Francisco airport yesterday. He'd flown in from North Platte, where the wrangling over his grandfather's estate "was just getting started" a month after the Judge's funeral. Hope had talked him into coming out for a long weekend and a break from all that.

"It gets crowded sometimes," Hope explained. "In the summer, on warm days."

"Golfers are snobs," Danny added. "They won't travel here to play because it's a short nine-hole course with plain greens, no fancy bunkers, and grass that isn't manicured daily by a team of horticulturists. So it's not a 'destination,' it's just part of town. There are a lot of little courses like this in Scotland, where the locals play."

"That sounds fantastic," Dylan said.

"We're going to SCOTLAND!" Gabriel chimed in with his best Braveheart accent. "With Uncle BISON!"

"You are?" Dylan replied. "That's great! To play golf?"

"Yeah," Danny added. "Bison's never been to Scotland! Can you imagine that? Guy's been a pro golfer for the better part of twenty years! He's won on tour! I was amazed when he told us that. So later this summer we're all going to spend a week in Dornoch. You should come!" He laughed. "Unless of course Big Poppa gets his magic cane firing on all cylinders before that and we go watch Bison win the Open instead!"

"That seems pretty unlikely," Dylan said, shaking his head. He looked at Hope. "I don't know how much you've heard from your father, but it looks like the odds of any more of the Judge's money going his way are pretty slim."

"Good," Hope said. "The sooner he gives up on that crazy cane the better." She looked at Danny. "We've been trying to think of something better for him to do," she said, "but it has to be his idea. He'd never be happy marching to someone else's beat. That makes it tough. We've thrown a few things out, but nothing's hooked him yet."

"And Bison's been playing pretty well on his own," Danny added. "He got into the last two Web.com tournaments, after his good finish in Houston. He made both cuts! He's got a regular caddie, a Scottish guy who's a real veteran. I think he's going to be able to play a bunch of events this summer, have a really solid year!"

They reached the edge of the fairway, where Peter's sand wedge off the corner of the tarmac had come to rest about 330 yards short of the green. Peter looked at Gabriel, who was making more faces at Irwin. Peter smiled and took out his driver. "OK, Gabriel, since you hit my shot from there, I'm hitting it from here!"

Gabriel laughed and watched as Peter took a huge swing and launched a low bullet down the runway. They saw it take a big skip off the pavement, then another, before rolling out towards the end of the runway and the green beyond. "Great shot!" Danny said. Gabriel ran up and slapped Peter's hand.

"Show off!" Veeka added, laughing. "That was awesome!"

"Thanks," Peter said, smiling at Gabriel as he took Irwin's scooter and they headed down the fairway.

"I'm very jealous," Dylan told Hope. "You're out

here all the time with these trick shot artists while I'm back there with the lawyers and bookkeepers, maybe getting nine holes in at River's Edge a few times a week. Thank you for getting me out here!"

"It's great to see you! Is it taking longer in North Platte than you expected?" Hope asked.

"Yes and no," Dylan replied. "It's certainly going to be longer than I thought it would when I left New York. I've already had to make some arrangements there, move some things around, talk about bringing in a new associate lawyer." He laughed. "I'm sure Judge Smails would love it if his estate created a job opportunity for a young LGBTQ lawyer in New York City! But no, it's not going to take that much longer than I figured it would after Dr. Turin confessed and I learned about all of the Judge's money."

"Why would that make it more complicated or take longer?" Peter asked. "Does who killed him make a difference, on the estate side of it?"

"It can," Dylan told him. "If Ivanka had killed him, for example, she couldn't have inherited anything. Here, even though Dr. Turin didn't inherit anything himself, he was involved with the Judge and his main beneficiaries, Kellerman and Postlewaite, in financing the use of the cane to affect the results of the Houston Open. Or, to put it another way, the murderer was part of a criminal conspiracy with the two main beneficiaries of the Judge's will."

"Even if their macdohickey never worked?" Danny asked.

"Right," Dylan nodded. "It doesn't matter so much as long as there's an overt act and criminal intent. If you're part of a conspiracy to bust into Fort Knox with a tank, you can't get off the hook because your tank ran out of gas on the way to the vault. But the crazy thing here is that the whole conspiracy with the cane—that was chicken feed compared to the real money Kellerman and Postlewaite had been laundering through all the Judge's different businesses for years!"

"That's why Smails told Poppa they'd kill them if they found out about it," Hope said.

Dylan nodded again. "The last thing Kellerman and Postlewaite wanted was for Smails to get involved in some minor league flimflammery like that and have it blow up on them like this."

"Which is why Smails took the money from his Bushwood guys," Danny said. "He didn't want Kellerman and Postlewaite to find out about it."

"But he was too cheap to risk that much of his own money," Dylan added. "And Tromble kept asking for more money. So the Judge wound up dragging Kellerman and Postlewaite into it anyway, hooking them together with his small town buddies in this goofy conspiracy to fix golf tournaments that wound up bringing down their ongoing multimillion dollar money laundering machine."

"So will all that be part of the criminal trial?" Hope asked. "What happens next?"

"I'm pretty sure there's not going to be any criminal trial," Dylan told her. "Not for murder at least. Dr. Turin and his lawyer will almost certainly take a plea bargain. It's just a question of how long he's going to spend in jail and whether he's going to name names."

"And then what?" Danny wondered. "Does all the rest of it wind up in the probate court?"

"It could," Dylan nodded. "But I hope it doesn't! What Mom and I are shooting for," he explained, "is a deal with Kellerman and Postlewaite. In exchange for her agreeing not to challenge the Judge's will on grounds that it was part of their money laundering conspiracy, a way for them to insure they'd reap the benefits of their crimes, they'd agree to give us a big chunk of the Judge's money."

"And there wouldn't be any criminal charges?" Hope asked. "For their money laundering?"

"That's up to the district attorney," Dylan said. "Not us." He paused. "But it's probably safe to say that it's more likely that they'd face charges if we did challenge the will on those grounds."

"So they'll make a deal with you," Danny concluded.

"I expect so," Dylan nodded. "But probably not until after Dr. Turin gets sentenced, so he can't upset anyone's apple cart."

"So they're still trying to keep him from talking?"

"For sure," Dylan agreed. "After you and Bison walked off Bushwood that morning, things slowed down for a few days, but since the Judge's funeral they've been talking. Probably Kellerman and Postlewaite will write a check to the dentist's family, write a bigger check to Mom, and wind up getting to keep a lot of their laundered money."

"That doesn't seem right," Hope commented.

"That everyone wins but the Bushwood guys?" Danny asked. "I don't know. Maybe there's some justice in that."

"Says the international multi-affiliated non-resident member!" Hope teased him, sticking her tongue out like Veeka.

"Oh, there's no justice in that!" Danny laughed. "But it does mean we can have Dylan out to play at Bushwood!"

"You're going back to North Platte?" Dylan waved his arm over the ocean. "And leaving this?"

"We'll be back here on weekends," Hope said.

"She's determined to keep the church going," Danny added. "It really makes a big difference for a lot of people here! And Gabriel still has five or six weeks of school left. But I'm trying to get back there at least once or twice a month, to see Dougie and Heidi. It's going to be hard for him, retiring. Not going to Bushwood every day, even though he probably will anyway, just to give lessons and hang out. We're taking them to Scotland too, later this summer."

Veeka and Hope hit their second shots and they all walked over to Gabriel's drive. "So what do I do now?" he asked.

Hope looked at Danny, who smiled back at her. "You've got to do what feels right," Danny told Gabriel. "You're about 225 yards from the front of the green. That's probably a little further than you can hit your three wood, unless you curve it right and bounce it off the runway again. But that's risky: your ball might not bounce off, and then you'd have to take a penalty. So you could do that. Or, you could try to hit it as far down the fairway as you could. Or, you could try to hit it 135 yards, which would leave you 90 yards, which is a distance where you've hit a lot of great wedge shots! Or you could do something else: you could try to hit it straight up in the air like Peter did or you could come up with some shot nobody's ever thought of before!"

"But we can't tell you which of those shots feels right to *you*," Hope said.

"It's one of those deals where the answer is whatever feels right inside," Peter added, taking Veeka's hand. "You'll do the best playing the shot you believe in the most." He looked at Veeka and smiled.

Gabriel looked them all over. "I believe it would be much easier if somebody just told me what to do!"

They all laughed. "Sure it would," Dylan told him.
"Today. But in the long run, it would just make you hate
playing golf with Danny, or your mom, if they started
telling you what to do on every shot. Does that really
sound like very much fun? Do you like it when your mom
tells you what to do?"

"NO!" Gabriel cried, laughing. He looked down the
fairway and examined his clubs, like he was figuring out
the distances. After a moment he took out his hybrid and
played a nice shot down the middle of the fairway. He got
a nice round of golf claps and they moved on.

Dylan and Danny were both able to go for the green
with their second shots, but neither of them was able to stop
their ball on the green. "That's OK!" Gabriel told them.
"You can feel good about your shots from there!"

www.ingramcontent.com/pod-product-compliance
Lightning Source LLC
Chambersburg PA
CBHW061509120726
48001CB00004B/1269